Whisked Away

June Whatley

ISBN: 978-1-952661-95-2

Outline

Chapter 1

Without Warning

The park swarmed with people decked out in party clothes. Two small, puffy clouds hung overhead and spied on the group from the azure morning sky. A cool gentle breeze wafted through the crowd, quite surprising for a summer day in the valley, creating the perfect atmosphere for an outdoor, Tennessee wedding.

Guests scurried toward the creek and gathered under the shade trees. Small children dabbled in the edge of the water, mostly against their mothers' wishes, but so much joy surrounded the festivities, even the pickiest moms refused to complain.

Shayla spotted the groom and paused to admire the scene. Late-middle-aged Thomas Phillips, nicknamed Philly, struck a very handsome figure in his light gray suit, white shirt, and blue vest. He fidgeted beside a big table-shaped rock next to the creek where he and his bride-to-be had their first date, four years ago to the day, just him and his beloved Candice.

Max, his best friend and best man, stood next to him. At varying intervals, their eyes darted toward the parking lot, awaiting the arrival of the bride.

"Ashy, I can hardly believe Mom's getting married today and I think it's so cute the way he calls her his filly."

Ashton chuckled. "Yep, Philly and his filly, he's definitely different."

Shayla giggled. "I know, right? And Mom loves him so much, he's such an awesome guy. I was afraid Mom would never be happy again after Dad died."

One of her brother's shoulders peaked toward his ear. "It doesn't seem like Dad's been gone seven years, I knew he would be next to impossible to replace, but Philly's top-notch for sure. I'm glad he and Max came into our lives. Can you believe it's been more than four years since they scooped up all those fake military guys in front of our house?"[i]

"Hey look, bubba, there's Bailey.[ii] She's waiting for you, you go on ahead, I'm going to dash into the Ladies' Room to check my hair and makeup."

"You're fine, Shay, just come on."

A long slow sigh escaped Shayla's lips. "A wedding in the park, it can't get much more romantic than this." Then she cut her eyes toward her brother, an air of urgency filling her voice. "You go ahead, Ashy. I want to look perfect, I'll only be a minute. Go on, Bailey's waving."

Shayla watched as Ashton trotted toward their friend. They had met Bailey five years ago and the smile on Ashton's face spoke volumes. That girl captured his heart by calling him Ash-boat, of all things. Shayla grinned, waved, then dashed into the facilities.

The light flickered on automatically, sandy soil scratched beneath her shoes on the concrete, but otherwise, the fresh smell gave testimony to a recent cleaning. A full-length mirror reflected sunlight streaming in through a high window, Shayla stepped before the long glass and smoothed her dress. Her eyes scanned upwards, but an unexpected surprise greeted her, the image of a stranger appeared, a dark-haired girl with terrified eyes stared back. "What?"

A shy, pitiful voice tremored. "Can you help me? Will you help me get out of here?" The girl lifted her hand.

Without hesitation Shayla reached, but instead of knuckles colliding with glass, her hand slipped straight through. "Take my hand!"

The frightened girl, much younger than her own seventeen years, grabbed hold. Shayla latched on and tugged, but rather than the young girl coming toward her, in a flash, Shayla lurched through the mirror into a dark, murky storeroom. "Wait! What? Where are we?"

The frightened girl pleaded, "How did that happen? Can you get us out?"

Shayla turned and stared at the wall behind her. "That mirror must hang over a travel portal, you somehow activated it from this side. I thought I could pull you out, but instead, I'm here with you." Shayla turned aside and placed her finger on her cheek. "This happened to me before when I grabbed Ashy's pant leg, rather than pulling him out, the vortex pulled me in."[iii]

"What? Who's Ashes?"

"Never mind, it's not important now, but we need to find a way out." Shayla reached toward the wall, which only seconds before had been glass, now a solid, opaque surface greeted her palm. "This is where I came through, but now the portal's closed." She turned to the young girl. "Who are you? And how'd you get here?"

"I'm Teressa, people call me Ressa."

"Where are we, Ressa?"

"I don't know. They brought me, four other girls and a little boy here in a van. I heard them say that we would only be here for one night and to make the most of us."

"What did they mean by make the most of you?"

"They sell us for an hour, or for the night, or we have to work in kitchens or clean bathrooms. The big man owns us and we have to do whatever he tells us to do, then the woman takes us to a place to work for the night. She said to think of it as a job and we'd be okay."

Shayla straightened. "Ressa, that's not okay. How long have they been making you do this?"

"I'm twelve now, I think, and I was about five when they took me."

"Five! Who took you? How did they take you?"

"They told me my momma sold me to the big man for enough money to get her next dose of drugs."

Shayla leaned forward and placed her palms on Ressa's shoulders, but feeling a flinch, she jerked her hands away. "I'm sorry, I didn't mean you any harm," then she realized how bad Ressa smelled. "How did you get here, right here in this closet, right now, I mean?"

"The woman fell asleep and I snuck her keys out of her pocket. The others were in a corner and were afraid to come with me, so I left. I hoped I could get out and bring help back for 'em. You are the only person that I've seen, I'm sure the woman'll wake up soon and she'll come looking for me with a belt."

"They whip you?"

Ressa lowered her chin and nodded. "If we

7

disobey or don't make the customers happy or it's worse when we try to run away, if you can't help me, that woman'll beat me sumthin' fierce. She's done it to some other girls and they had to be thrown out because they looked so bad. She said they couldn't afford to feed 'em, if they didn't make any money."

Shayla leaned forward. "That's horrible!"

The young girl peered into her eyes. "Actually, sometimes I think the girls who get thrown out are the lucky ones. That's why I took the chance tonight, if I can't escape, maybe they'll at least make me look bad enough that they'll throw me out. Sometimes the customers beat girls up and they have to throw them out too. Most of the girls don't last very long. I don't know why they've had me so many years, but tonight is the first time I've tried to run away, so maybe I'll get lucky tonight."

Looking into the young girl's eyes, Shayla tried to comfort her. "You're with me now and we'll find a way out of here. Okay?"

Tired eyes greeted Shayla's with a smile. "That'd be great, ma'am."

"Call me Shayla, or Shay, for short. May I hold your hand?"

A small grubby palm reached toward her. Shayla took hold and gently wrapped her fingers around the frail hand. "Let's pray." Shayla closed her eyes. "Dear Heavenly Father, the fact that I'm here is no surprise to you. Please help me to get Ressa and the others safely out of here. Give me wisdom and strategy and keep us safe from harm. In Jesus' name, amen."

The young girl peered up. "Who were you talking to? Did you see your father?"

"No, I was praying, don't you know about praying?"

Ressa's head twisted side-to-side.

A smile crept across Shayla's face and she whispered, "I was talking to the King of the Universe and asking him to keep us safe."

Again, the small head wobbled back and forth. "I don't know who that is."

"Well, he created the world and all that's in it, including you and me."

Ressa tightened her lips. "I wish he hadn't."

Shayla's eyebrows rose and her mouth dropped open, but what could she say to a young girl who'd been abused and mistreated like this? She whispered another prayer. "Abba give me words."

Into her spirit came wisdom. "Safety first, words later."

Shayla stepped to the door and cracked it open. "Let's see where we are." A dingy hallway lay before them. "Which way did you come from?"

Ressa's free hand pointed.

Shayla glanced the opposite direction. "Okay, then we'll go this way. Be as quiet as a mouse, okay?"

The young girl nodded.

They slid along the wall trying to stay hidden in the dim, dank corridor. Shayla shivered, her short sleeves offered little comfort in the damp mustiness.

She knew each door they approached could mean freedom or danger. She paused at the first door and laid her ear to the grimy wood. No sound came from the room, enticing her to turn the knob. The door slid inwards, the squeak, though minimal, sounded deafening in the hallway. She peeked inside, a stale smell assaulted her nose.

Shayla pulled Ressa in behind her, closed the door and tiptoed across the room, the newspaper covered windows still offered some light. She tried each one, but with no success, they'd been nailed shut. She looked for a mirror on an interior wall, hoping to find a portal. Her fingertips became scratched as she dragged them across some boards in search of an exit. Finding no way of escape, she opened the door again, but heard voices. She pulled back inside and twisted the center part of the knob to the locked position.

A woman's voice bleated-out like a sheep. "I don't know where she is, but she couldn't have gone far."

The man's voice, sounded gruff, as though damaged by smoking and liquor. "I can't believe the little whelp tried to escape, after all we've done for her all these years. She'll pay for this."

The woman added. "This is a bad example for the others."

Their voices faded down the hall, jiggling doorknobs as they passed.

When the noise had abated, Shayla once again slipped the door open and pulled her new charge into the hallway behind her. Knowing the direction that the two kidnappers had gone, she doubled back past the closet where they had met and down the corridor from which Ressa had first come. "Maybe there's another way out, down here."

"I don't think there is, I looked for one. That's how I ended up in the storeroom and then I saw you."

After trying each door, Shayla turned one knob and the door swung inward. Five young, dirty faces cowered in a corner.

Ressa's raised finger pointed. "See, this is where they keep us."

With her free hand, Shayla beckoned. "Kids, come with us. Please, we have to go!"

No one moved, but their faces reacted.

So distracted, she hadn't heard the light footsteps creeping up behind her.

"Well, well, what have we here? A princess is a crisp, blue party dress."

Shayla spun around to find herself confronted by a woman of wide girth, with a snaggle-toothed grin, and dirty clothes staring back at her.

The woman glared at Shayla. "I see you've returned our merchandise." She glanced at Ressa. "You'll pay for running away, girl."

Shayla leapt to her defense. "It wasn't her fault. I saw you sleeping and I slipped in and took her out. Isn't that right, Ressa?"

The girl's eyes stared at the floor.

Shayla shook the girl's arm. "Ressa, isn't that right?"

She nodded slowly.

"It doesn't matter, princess, she'll be punished for letting you haul her outta here and you'll take her place while she heals up enough to see customers again."

The woman backed her way through the door and slammed it shut behind her. "Jackson, Jackson, I've got her back and a bonus too."

The gruff voiced man propelled the door open and stormed in, a wide leather belt in his hand.

Shayla stepped in front of Ressa.

The man strode forward. "You think you're gonna stop me, do you? Well, you've got another think coming." The man swished the belt high over his head, but at that instant a piece of newspaper fluttered from the corner of the window. Bright light streamed in and hit the man square in the eyes like a laser beam. "Ow, ow, my eyes!" He backed away rubbing them and retreated from the room shouting, "This ain't over!" And he slammed the door behind him.

A long burst of air escaped from Shayla's lips. "Thank you, Abba! Please give me wisdom and help me get these kids out of here." She turned to face Ressa. "Are you alright?"

"I guess so, but he'll be back and he'll be madder than ever. How did you make the paper come off the window? It's glued on real hard, I've tried to scratch it off, but couldn't."

Shayla bent slightly to Ressa's ear level and whispered, "It wasn't me, it was God."

"Who?"

Straightening with a jerk, Shayla asked, "You've never heard the name, God, before?"

"Only when people cuss."

"I'm so sorry, Ressa, I'll explain when I get you out of here."

Then the door flung open again. The woman pushed her weight through the opening. "Jackson wants you, Ressa."

The young girl stood with wide eyes, Shayla pulled her close. "I don't think so."

"Then you can come with her too, princess."

Shayla shook her head. "No!"

"You can come quietly or," a tiny flick of light and the crackle of a taser split the air, "or I can have fun getting you there. Now are you coming or not?"

The woman backed through the doorway, Ressa

and Shayla followed and marched down the hall.

"Stop, here." The woman turned a knob and pushed the door open, put her hand on Shayla's back and gave her a shove. She stumbled in and Ressa staggered in behind her. The room was dirty and stank, a bed with filthy sheets stood in front of them.

Jackson growled, "Which one first?"

Shayla pulled Ressa tight to her side. "You're not going to touch either one of us."

Jackson threw his head back and laughed. "We'll see about that, Little Miss Mouth."

He lunged toward them, but Shayla jerked Ressa back and they both collided with the wall next to the closed door. Air began to spin, dizziness swirled inside her head, Shayla thought she was about to faint, but instead, the wall became spongey and they both fell through and floated onto a clean stone floor.

Chapter 2

Marble Must Be Better

A dazzling white marble floor and clean light gray walls delighted their eyes. Shayla and Ressa pushed onto their elbows, scrambled to a seated position, then onto their knees.

As she stood, Shayla helped Ressa. "Huh, this has got to be better, right?"

The girl looked around, but hesitated to commit to any answer. "It smells better, that's for sure."

A mirror hung above a small wall table, Shayla fluffed her tresses. "Look at my hair! What is Mom going to think when she sees me?"

Ressa's face jerked toward Shayla's image. "You've got a Momma?"

Wide eyes turned toward Ressa. "Well, yes."

She centered her gaze on Shayla's smooth face and asked, "And she didn't sell you?"

Tears filled Shayla's eyes, she glanced away.

"Uh, no, she didn't, but we need to find some help."

A door opened at the far end of the hall, a tall lean woman in a lovely business suit, stepped into the corridor.

Shayla spun in her direction. "Excuse me! Can you help us?"

The woman jumped, then when she saw the two girls standing at the other end of the long hallway, she scurried toward them, high heels clicking. "What are you doing out here? Did you displease your guest? Why are you both such a mess?" She towed them toward a luxurious bathroom. "Get in here." Pushing a brush at Shayla, she fussed, "Take this and fix your hair. Hurry, the gentlemen are on an hourly rate. And you," she grabbed Ressa by the arm. "You come in here and take a shower. You stink. I'll get you some fresh clothes."

Shayla nodded at Ressa and pointed toward the shower. "Go ahead, I'll be right here."

"What do I use?"

Shayla pulled the door open wide and pointed. "That bottle is for your hair. Wet your hair first, then put a little of that liquid in your hand and rub it onto your scalp."

"What's it supposed to do?"

"It will make bubbles to clean your hair."

Ressa stepped in and a few seconds later, she tossed her clothes out.

Shayla pushed the door shut and the water came

on.

A concerned voice erupted over the noise of the shower. "It's not working. There aren't any bubbles."

"Well, rinse it out and do it again, maybe your hair is too oily to suds-up."

Water splashed, then the worried voice came again. "Okay, there're a few bubbles."

"Rinse it out and do it again."

A moment later. "Now what?"

Shayla sheepishly asked, "Is it okay if I take a look?"

"Sure, why not?"

Shayla cracked the door and laughed when she saw a mound of shampoo suds about five inches high on Ressa's head. "Now rinse it all out."

"Why do you put it in, then wash it out?"

"It's to clean your hair, like you clean your clothes."

"We don't clean our clothes. We usually wear 'em till they tear up. That's the only time we get more clothes."

Sadness flooded Shayla's spirit, she fought back tears. "Do you know what to do with the soap?

"Is that the hard cake that smells so good?"

"Yes, that's it. Take the wash cloth hanging on the hook, wet it and rub the soap on it, then wash your whole face and body with the sudsy cloth."

A few seconds later, Ressa asked, "Like this?"

Shayla peaked in and saw streaks of soap and dirt on Ressa's face. "Do you mind if I help?"

The girl shrugged her shoulders. "No, I don't mind."

Shayla pushed the showerhead toward the wall, stepped in and washed Ressa's face, neck, and back. "Here, take the cloth and wash the rest of your body, including your private parts."

Ressa's head tipped to the side, her eyes scrunched together. "Which parts are private, Shay?"

Shayla nearly burst into tears, but regained her composure and explained, then said, "Now, when you're all done, rinse away all of the soap. Make sure you get it all off, private parts too."

Seconds later. "Now what?"

"Turn the water off." Shayla handed in a towel. "Wrap this around you and step out here." Shayla took another towel to dry Ressa's hair, then reached for a wide tooth comb to groom the beautiful black hair and remove the tangles. She turned her around and looked. "My goodness, you are so pretty, Ressa."

Wide eyes stared up at her. "I am?"

"Come and look."

Shayla turned the clean face toward the mirror, Ressa was astonished. "Is that me?"

"Yes, that's you, let me dry your hair and look, the lady brought you some clean clothes."

Several minutes later, Shayla spun Ressa toward a full-length mirror. "This is the new Ressa."

The reflection of beautiful black hair, deep brown eyes, a soft flowing red dress and black patent leather shoes greeted the girl. "That can't be me!"

"Who do you think it is?"

"Another girl like you, when I first saw you through the window. Do you think she can help us?"

Shayla pointed at the image. "Talk to the girl in the mirror."

"Hi, I'm Ressa, my friend Shayla and I need your help. Can you help us to get out of here?" Her eyes flew open wide. "Those words are coming out of her mouth, I mean my mouth. That *is* me!"

Shayla placed her hands on Ressa's shoulders. "Yes, it is and you're beautiful."

Tears puddled in the rims of the young girl's eyes. "Is this what Mommas are supposed to do for you?"

Shayla cleared her throat and pushed the sadness from her own voice. "Yes, that's part of it, but they do a lot more too."

The door jerked open. "Are you two finished?"

Shayla stepped aside and turned Ressa toward the lady.

"My, my, what a change. Yes, I think the new

gentleman will like you."

Shayla stepped in front of her again. "No, ma'am, she finished."

"She's finished when I say she's finished, young lady. And you will do quite well for his friend, Senior Roberto."

"No! Would you do this to your daughter? And we're staying together."

"I don't have a daughter, stupid, but I'll ask the gentlemen if it will be okay if you two stay together."

Chapter 3

Marble Isn't Better

Moments later, the door flew open again.

"You are in luck, girly. The gentlemen were fine with you both being in the room. It will probably be a contest of male superiority, but you asked for it." The woman led them to a luxurious bedroom. "Wait here and you two had better perform for your guests or it will be the darkroom for you both." The door slammed behind her.

Within seconds, two distinguished-looking men entered the room. At first, they said nothing, but both looked at the girls and walked around them. Finally, one spoke and introduced himself, "I'm Mr. Smith," then pointed to his friend and introduced him as Roberto Jones. "Which do you choose, Roberto? I'll give you first choice, my friend. Do you prefer the black straight hair or the curls?"

"I'm partial to the red dress." His eyes sparkled

as he stared at Ressa.

Shayla stepped in front of her. "No way!"

Roberto laughed. "So, are you choosing me, curly-top?" and he winked at his friend.

Shayla folded her arms across her mid-section. "No, we are not doing this!"

Roberto scowled. "Did the lady tell you that we wanted resistance? Or what game are you playing?"

"I'm playing no game! Would you want your daughter, or wife, or sister, or mother to be treated like this? Think about what you are doing!"

Roberto spread his hands. "But you chose this life, why complain now?"

Shayla leaned forward. "We did *not* choose this? Ressa was sold by her mother at age five, or at least that's the lie they've been telling her for seven years."

Ressa stepped to the side and cut her eyes toward Shayla's face. "Do you think it was a lie?"

"Yes, I think it could've been. They lie, they cheat, they abuse; they are wicked people. Mr. Roberto, do you want to take advantage of this poor innocent girl? You would be in a long line of sleazy men who did? Think of your wife, or mother, or sister. What would you want the man in your place to do? Please don't do this."

His arms flapped out to his sides, then down again. "But we've paid."

Shayla balled her fists and plopped them on her

waist. "Is your money worth more than your soul?"

Roberto's eyebrows knit together. "Now you sound like my mother."

Shayla tilted her chin up. "She was right. It sounds like she was an honorable woman. What would she want you to do? Wouldn't she want you to be an honorable man?"

The other man broke in. "I don't care what you decide to do, Roberto, but I'm getting my money's worth," and he glared at the girls.

In a flash, Shayla jerked her hands away from her waist and pointed her palms out toward him. "NO! In the name of Jesus Christ, Father God and his Holy Spirit! You will not touch us."

The man tipped his head back and laughed with hideous glee. "Watch me!" He took a step forward and the grin melted from his face. He looked like someone had thrown cold water on him. His legs went limp and he crumbled to the floor.

Roberto stared at him, then glanced toward Shayla who stood stone-faced and tight-lipped. Roberto shouted, "What have you done?"

"I have called upon the almighty God whom I serve and the one you should serve too. You are a decent man who has been led astray by the lust of your flesh. Leave now and repent of your sins and take us out of this place."

His face turned white, he grabbed the door knob, yanked it inward and fled, leaving the girls standing in the luxurious room.

Ressa looked up. "He left us."

Shayla faced her and smiled. "It's okay, God hasn't left us."

The woman in the pretty suit ran into the room and saw the man in the floor. "What have you done?"

Once again, Shayla's fists flew to her hips. "I've told him the truth. Roberto fled, but this man resisted."

"What truth?"

Shayla shouted, "That what you are doing here is wicked! This young girl was told that her mother sold her and she has been exploited for seven years! Now let us go."

The woman hardened her face. "I can't help what others have done, but I have a business to run. Now what did you do to this man?"

Shayla relaxed her hands at her waist. "Perhaps you should call an ambulance if you think he's injured."

The woman's eyes flew open wide. "But that would be terrible for business."

Shayla folded her arms again. "What do you do when a customer hurts a girl?"

The woman's blank face started back. "We call the doctor that we have on staff."

"Then maybe you should call him." Shayla whispered under her breath, "Abba, what am I to do? I need your guidance."

She heard in her spirit. "Stand still and see the goodness of the Lord."

From beside her, Ressa looked up and asked, "What did that bird say?"

Shayla whipped her head toward her young charge. "You saw him?"

Ressa nodded. "He whispered sumthin in your ear."

A moment later the woman opened the door and ushered in an elderly man. "Doctor, I don't know what they did to him, but I found him like this."

The old man leaned over the man lying on the floor. "Maybe it was a heart attack. Let me examine him." He looked up at the girls. "What was going on when he collapsed?"

Shayla squared her shoulders. "I told him that he would not touch us, in the name of the Lord, but he stepped forward anyway, then he collapsed."

The doctor chuckled and knelt to examine the man. "Well, sweetie, I imagine you scared the daylights out of him."

Shayla leaned toward the doctor. "You also need to repent. You know what they do here and you help them. That's wicked and God will not allow you to go unpunished."

The doctor laughed, but when he touched the man on the floor, he fell in a heap on top of him.

The woman screamed. "Willard, Duncan, come

here immediately!"

Through the doorway burst two burly men. "Take these girls to the basement and lock them in."

The two approached.

Shayla expected them to crumble to the floor too, but instead, each of them grabbed Shayla by an arm and Duncan reached back for Ressa. They towed them down the hallway and onto some stairs.

At least it was clean and bright.

At the bottom of the stairs, the men shoved the girls into a room, turned off the light and shut the door. A key turned in the lock on the other side.

Now only a sliver of light inched in under the door, a few seconds later—*click* and complete darkness surrounded them.

Air moved around Shayla as Ressa swished her hands in the air searching for her new friend.

"I'm right here." Shayla reached and two hands grasped her arm. "Come here, little one."

A startled voice asked, "Why did you call me that?"

Shayla shrugged her shoulders, but in the dark, only she knew. "I don't know, it just popped out, why?'

"I remember someone calling me that before I was taken away."

"Do you think it was your Momma?"

"Maybe, I think so."

Shayla sought permission. "Is it okay if I call

you that?"

Ressa sweet, calm voice answered. "Yeah, it made me feel kinda warm inside."

She pulled the girl close. "Okay, then 'little one' it is."

Ressa asked, "What do we do now?"

Shayla slid her hand into Ressa's. "We pray."

"Is that when you talk to the bird?"

Shayla couldn't help but giggle. "I'm actually talking to God; the dove is his Holy Spirit. I can't see him anymore, but I know he's there when I need him."

"But what can a bird do?"

She clutched Ressa's warm palm in hers. "Let's ask." Standing in the pitch-black darkness, Shayla raised her free hand. "Abba Father, what do you want us to know or what do you want us to do? I trust you, but we are truly in a dark mess," she chuckled, "as you can plainly see. Give me wisdom and direction. In Jesus' name. Amen."

A light the size of a pinpoint appeared at the back of the room.

As the luminous spot grew, Shayla watched Ressa's eyes widen. "What is it?"

"I don't know yet, we'll have to wait and see."

Then a voice spoke from beyond the brightness. "Come this way for a while, ladies, though your journey isn't finished yet."

Shayla stepped toward the light, pulling Ressa

behind her and spoke into the opening. "Abba, my mother is getting married today and I don't want to miss it."

A familiar soothing voice replied, "Trust me, Mighty One."

The opening grew wider and Shayla stepped through, Ressa followed close behind still clutching her hand. "Where are we now, Shay?"

Chapter 4

Into the Light

The familiar, soothing voice greeted them in a room flooded with light. "Shayla, I've brought you two here, because I want Teressa to come to know Me."

The light began to soften and the sound of water bubbling up greeted their ears. White marble with gold trim encircled the floor and a ceiling covered with gold glittered above them.

Ressa's shoulders reached for her ears. "Are we back upstairs in the marble house?"

Shayla leaned toward Ressa. "No, little one, this is the throne room of the King." She pointed. "That's Him, the older man seated on the throne."[iv]

"Has He bought us?"

"Not like you are thinking, but His Son, has paid a high price for our freedom."[v]

"What do we have to do for Him?"

"All we have to do is to believe that the King is real." She pointed again. "And you can see Him right there."

Ressa nodded. "He seems real."

Nodding in agreement, Shayla said, "Oh, He is. And you need to believe that He sent His Son to die in your place for your sins."[vi]

"What sins do I have? Do you mean what the men make us do?"

The King gently moved His head side-to-side. "No, little one, not what you were made to do against your will. That sin is on the ones who forced you, but have you ever thought bad things about your mother, because you thought she sold you?"

Ressa stared at the floor. "I hated her for doing it. Now Shayla says that maybe she didn't even do it, but I've hated the ones who made me do those ugly things too."

Shayla lifted Ressa's chin. "I can understand that, but now I want you to ask the King to forgive you of the hatred you've felt."

Ressa jerked away, fierce eyes stared at Shayla. "But they were wrong!"

Shayla bent toward her young charge. "Yes, little one, they were wrong, but forgiving them is *not* saying that they were right. Forgiveness sets you free from them and it allows God," she pointed at the King, "to deal with them. Holding on to unforgiveness is really saying that you want to continue feeling the anger and the hurt, you want to keeping feeling the way you do. I know that's not what you want, so now, I want you to set yourself free by forgiving those people and asking Abba to forgive you for hating them, then ask Him to take care of those wicked people. Will you do that?"

She nodded her head and turned toward the King, but her eyes faced the floor. "Mister, would you …"

But the King stopped her. "Teressa, my dear. Look at Me please. You have nothing to fear from Me and nothing to be ashamed of, lift your eyes and look at Me."

Inch-by-inch Ressa tipped her face up.

"That's better my lovely child and call Me, Abba. It is like calling me Daddy."

"Abba, I'm sorry I hated those people," her voice quickened, "but if You knew what they made me …"

The King lifted his hand and interrupted again. "I do know, child, and I'm so sorry for how they hurt you. Rest assured, vengeance is mine and they will not get away without facing My judgement.[vii] Unless they turn from their wicked ways, it would be better for them if they had tied a millstone around their necks and thrown themselves into the sea.[viii] Now try again, please."

"Yes, sir, Abba, I'm sorry for hating those people and for trying to run away."

A warm smile crossed the King's face. "No, Ressa, the trying to run away from the wicked people was fine, but when you ran away from your mother, you placed yourself in danger."

Ressa gasped. "I did what?" Her face reflected signs of searching her memory. "I did, didn't I? I remember now, running down the street, because I was mad at my momma, then a man and woman in a car stopped. They said they would take me where it was safe because my momma had sold me to them."

Shayla teared up and wrapped her arms around Ressa. "I'm so sorry, little one."

The King dipped His fingers into the water bubbling from beneath His throne.[ix]

Shayla knew what He wanted to do and guided Ressa toward him.

"Teressa, my dear, now the hardest part of all— I want you to forgive yourself for running away from your mother, for putting yourself in danger and for believing their lies. Will you do that for me?"

"But I don't deserve to forgive myself. I was stupid!"

"My dear, what I offer you is not because you deserve it, it's offered to you because I love you. You must forgive yourself, or the enemy will constantly attack your mind. Will you do that for Me?"

"If you show me how, Abba, I will and I'll forgive those bad people too."

"Come here, my dear."

She stepped forward.

Abba touched her head with the healing water on his fingertips. "Now child, know that I love you and you are forgiven. Your past is wiped away. Today you are clean like fresh, new snow.ˣ Anytime you need another touch of my healing, just ask me and believe that I want to give you healing. As proof, look at my Son's hands."

The man on the throne next to him, stretched his hands toward her.

"Oooo, that looks like it hurt."

Abba answered her. "It was very painful, my dear, but I sent him to die on the cross in your place, so you can have freedom from sin."

Ressa stared into his face. "But how could you do that to your son?"

"My only other choice was to allow sweet children like you to die, then suffer for eternity." The King paused, then said, "Now I want you to ask my Son—Jesus," he glanced to his right, "to forgive you and to come into your heart and live there."

With the question already written on her face, she asked, "But how can he do that?"

A dove appeared next to the King. "This is my Spirit. It is he who does the work and allows my Son into your heart."

Ressa scanned the three faces, first Abba's, then to the dove, finally to the Son. "Thank you for doing that for me. And Jesus will you forgive me and come into my heart and live there forever?"

Abba leaned forward and placed His elbows on His knees. "It is done! Now Teressa, I want you to go with Shayla and she will guide you, but you must go back into the dark room until you find the way of escape."

Eager, searching eyes greeted his gaze. "Can't we stay with You?"

"No, but My Spirit will be with you, fear not and trust Shayla, she has a deep love for you."

At that moment, Shayla realized she *did* love Ressa.

Ressa looked from the King to Shayla and back again. "I don't exactly understand, but I'll do what You ask me to."

The King nodded. "That is all that I can ask, sweet child." He leaned back on his throne. "Now both of you sit down, eat some figs and bread and drink some water." He handed them each a silver chalice. "It will be awhile before you are given food again, but this will sustain you."

They ate until they were filled, then Abba said, "Ladies, close your eyes."

They closed their eyes and it felt as if darkness began to swallow them. Shayla reached for Ressa's hand. "Are you okay?"

"I'm okay as long as you and Abba are with me."

Even though it was too dark to see her face, Shayla heard the peace and the smile in Ressa's voice. She pulled her close and they both slept in comfort on the floor of their cell.

***

Hours later, maybe even a day, the light flipped on in the stairwell. A sliver of light under the door called Shayla to sit up and she pulled Ressa up with her. She gave her a hug and smoothed her hair.

The door flung open, Duncan stepped in and pushed some bread and cheese at them. "Are you girls hungry?"

Shayla looked over at Ressa. "I am a little hungry, are you?"

She nodded. "A little bit, thanks."

Duncan's mouth flew open wide and his eyes stared from one face to the other. "Usually the girls are starving and nearly knock me over to get to the food."

Shayla reached for the bread and cheese and shared it with Ressa. "Thank you for thinking of us, Duncan. May I ask you a question?"

"Look, I don't know nuthin about nuthin. You can't get any information outta me."

Shayla smiled up at him. "No, not a question like that?"

"What then?"

"Why are you doing this work? You don't seem like Willard. You're different."

"I use to be … never mind." The volume of his voice rose. "I don't want to talk about it."

The Spirit nudged Shayla again.

Ressa glared at Duncan and said, "Ooo, you're in trouble now. That bird is talking to her in her ear."

Chapter 5

The Dove

An uncontrollable giggle burst from Shayla. "No, Ressa, Duncan isn't in trouble, in fact you two have more in common than you would think."

Ressa's eyebrows drew close together. "Really? What-cha you mean?"

"Duncan was a runaway and he was living on the street, selling himself for food, money and places to sleep."

His shoulders jumped back. "How'd you …. Who told you that?"

Ressa stared up at the gigantic guy. "I told you, you were in trouble. Every time that bird whispers to her, somebody gets blasted."

"Not blasted, Ressa. Abba wants us to help him."

Duncan folded his arms and tipped his chin up.

"Help me! I don't need no help. You two are the ones that are locked in the dark room."

Shayla glanced up at him. "That's not what the dove said. He told me that you are a wounded frightened little boy inside. He says that in your emotions, you never grew past ten-years-old. That's the first time a man took advantage of you. You were hungry and cold, sitting in a bus-stop shelter and it was raining hard. A man offered to give you a ride, to help you get warm and to give you something to eat. You were very hungry then, that's why you brought us food, isn't it?"

Duncan stared at the floor.

"You were also hungry for love, so you trusted the man. He took care of you at first, but you had to earn your way through sleeping with him, then when you started growing and looking like a man, he didn't want you anymore and the Madame in the suit doesn't know you are here, does she?"

Tears streaked down Duncan's face. "How did you know that? I'm so ashamed."

Ressa rose to her knees. "You don't have to be ashamed; you need to meet Abba. He can heal all of your hurts."

Shayla's faced whipped toward the young girl.

Ressa scrunched her eyebrows and asked, "Isn't that right?"

"Yes, it is, did you hear that inside?"

Ressa smiled and nodded, yes, as she nibbled

her cheese and bread.

Shayla patted the floor. "Sit down here with us, Duncan and let us tell you about the King."

"Who?"

"Have you ever heard of God?"

"Yeah, when I was a kid, but he's never done anything for me."

"Yes, he has and we can tell you about it, can't we Ressa?" They both smiled and Ressa nodded.

Duncan left the door open and sat across from the girls, inside the room.

About two hours later, they ended with a prayer where Duncan asked Jesus to forgive him of his sins and come into his heart to be Lord of his life. A different man stood up and faced the girls. "I'll go up and try to get them to bring you upstairs," but about that time the door at the top of the stairs burst open.

A gruff man's voice disrupted the quiet with a shout. "Duncan!"

Shayla whispered, "Don't be afraid, you are a man and you can make your own way now. Don't let him bully you."

"I'm here, Willard, what do you want?"

"Get your fat rump up here."

Shayla leaned toward him and whispered, "You've got this, Duncan. Abba is with you. Listen with your heart."

Duncan walked very deliberately up the steps,

the girls snuck out of the room, to the bottom of the stairway and watched.

Willard drew back and swung at Duncan's head, but Duncan's hand shot-up and caught the hand before it contacted his face. "Willard, you will never slap me again." He leaned his face in close. "Do you hear me?"

Too stunned to talk, Willard backed away.

Through clenched teeth, Duncan said, "Good, now take me to Madame."

Shayla and Ressa glanced at each other, their mouths dropped open wide, they jerked their hands up to stifle the giggles.

Then Ressa whispered, "Abba healed him good, didn't he, Shay?"

They finished their bread and cheese then looked around for a bathroom. A metal can sat in the corner with a partial roll of toilet paper perched on its lid. "I guess this will have to do," said Shayla. "I really need to go."

Ressa stood in front of her with her back turned to give her privacy. "Sometimes they call them 'Susie Cans,' sometimes they just call them 'the can,' for obvious reasons," then she giggled. "You know Shay, before I met you, I don't think I had ever laughed."

Shayla knew the reason. "It's the joy of the Lord that's with you now. You became a follower of the Lord and you received His word, *in much affliction* and you got the joy of the Holy Spirit with it.[xi] Or that's close to what the scripture says. Anyway, that's what happened to you. You got the joy of the Lord."

"What's scritture?"

Shayla explained. "Scripture, it's Abba's words written down for you and me."

"Will you read some to me someday?"

Shayla stepped in front of Ressa. "Can't you read?"

"No, they said for me to do what they needed me to do, reading would only get me into trouble." She turned to use the can.

Shayla pressed her lips together and balled her hands into fists. "They knew that if you could read, they wouldn't be able to control you, you'd learn to be independent."

The door at the top of the stairs swung open. The woman's voice came out harsh. "Girls! Upstairs, now."

Chapter 6

One Uptight Woman

When they reached the top of the stairs, Madame's face was red and her hands were wadded into fists stacked on her waist. "Girls, what did you do to Duncan?"

Shayla folded her arms. "We didn't do anything to him."

Madame leaned forward at the waist. "Then why did he quit and storm out?"

From behind Shayla, Ressa laughed. "Because Abba splashed him good."

"What do you mean, someone 'splashed him,' who is Abba and how did he get in here?"

Ressa giggled. "He's the King of the Universe. He can heal you too. Do you want him to heal you?"

The woman straightened. "Heal me of what, you foolish girl?"

Ressa's voice came out very soft. "The hurts and the pain in your heart and in your head from when you were sold, like me. You swore an oath to yourself that no one would ever control you again, that you would always be the one in charge."

Madame's eyebrows jumped up and her eyes flew open wide. "How did you know that?"

"Abba says that you could have been in business or in leadership or anything, but you were afraid to move to something outside what you had always known, but it's not too late to change. You need to ask Abba to forgive you and ask His Son into your heart, then He will show you a new way."

The shocked woman turned and ran down the hall, her high heels clicking as she shouted, "Willard! Willard!"

Shayla took Ressa by the wrist. "That was awesome! I'm glad you can hear Abba, but now we need to run."

Ressa stared up at her. "Where to?"

Shayla stopped, her shoulders dropped and she turned to face her young friend. "I don't know, little one, I just don't know. We need to pray. Abba, we need your help. We don't know where to go or what to do. Show us, please. In Jesus' name. Amen."

As they lifted their eyes, three doors in the hallway drifted open.

Ressa pointed. "I think we're supposed to go there."

They headed down the hall.

Behind the first door was a young Asian girl. She was pretty, but her eyes reflected fear.

Ressa raised both hands and made a scooping motion, then whispered, "Come with us," but the girl didn't move.

She shook her head. "The woman will hurt me."

Shayla reassured her. "No, come with us. We will get you out."

The girl moved toward them. When she reached the door, Shayla latched onto one wrist and Ressa gripped the other.

Shayla whispered, "What's your name?"

"Tina."

They worked their way to the next door. Inside, a young boy, cowered in the corner.

Shayla whispered again, "Come with us." And waved to motion him to the door, but he didn't move until he saw Tina.

She beckoned him. "Try, Teddy, please."

He fled into the hall. His bare feet flapping as he ran.

Ressa loosed her hold on Tina's hand and she reached for Teddy's.

Tina and Teddy grabbed hands and walked between Shayla and Ressa to the last door.

Shayla peaked in. A young girl sat on the floor at the end of the bed playing with toys. "Hello, little girl."

The child looked around, her eyes widened and sparkled. "Are you going to get me home?"

Shayla stood up straight, her shoulders squared and her eyebrows arched. "I'm going to try. How did you know?"

"A nice, old man with a bird on his shoulder told me you were coming and not to be afraid."

Ressa's eyebrows shot up. "Abba?"

The small girl smiled. "Yes, that was his name."

Ressa whispered to the little girl. "What's your name?"

"They call me, Peaches."

Shayla tiptoed in and offered her hand. "Well, Peaches, let's do what Abba said, okay?"

Peaches took the outstretched hand and stood, leaving the toys behind.

Shayla led the way. "We need to find the front door." They crept down a beautiful marble staircase, toward a lovely arched double door. "When we get out, we need to find a policeman and tell him about this house."

When they reached the door, Ressa was surprised that it eased in toward Shayla before she even touched the knob.

Shayla grinned. "Abba."

Without warning, Madame's voice screeched behind them. "Nooooo!"

Shayla pushed the three younger children out and yelled, "Run and take care of Peaches."

Tina and Teddy gripped the tiny girl's wrists and tore off down the steps. Then Willard hit the door with his shoulder and slammed it shut.

Madame grabbed Shayla and Ressa, then shouted to the man, "Go after the younger ones, Willard, hurry."

He flung the door open and Shayla caught a glimpse of Duncan at the bottom of the stairs, standing with the three children. The look in his eyes, stopped Willard cold.

Shayla knew the children would be safe now with him.

Madame kicked the door closed, leaving Willard frozen on the top step. She dragged Shayla and Ressa toward the stairs that led to the dark room. She hustled them down the steps, clinched her teeth tight and hissed at them. "I'll leave you down here until you rot!"

Ressa shook her head. "No, Abba will get us out."

Madame placed her hands on her hips. "Out of a locked room, in a locked basement, with no windows? Huh!" She maneuvered them to the door and pushed them in. The door slammed shut. The sound of a rusty key scrapped inside the lock. The clickety-click of high heels faded up the stairs and the light flicked off.

Ressa eased herself to the floor. "Here we are again. Why do you think Abba didn't let us escape too?"

Shayla slid her way down the wall to the floor. "Because our mission isn't over yet."

"What mission, Shay?"

"We have set three children free from slavery and Abba set Duncan free from emotional slavery. I thought I could get you out, but here we sit. We'll have to wait for our next instructions from the King."

Their door began to creak open, the room beyond was dark, but not as dark as the room where they sat. The girls stood and waited for their eyes to adjust. Barely enough light lingered to allow them to move around, but they stepped out in faith. In the middle of the room they found the rail of the stairs.

A voice came from behind them. "Don't go up. Walk toward the wall under the stairs."

Shayla took Ressa's hand as they followed the instruction.

The warm voice came again. "Now turn and face the steps."

When they did, a swirl of air opened in front of them.

Abba's voice directed. "Step through, Warriors."

In faith, Shayla stepped in, the vortex pulled Ressa through behind her.

Ressa's voice, thinned by the air, asked, "Where are we going?"

Chapter 7

Into the Fray

Shayla and Ressa popped into a dingy room. At first their heads spun inside, then they heard a man's voice and it snapped them into the moment.

"I told you what you were going to do, now do it!" He unbuckled his belt and jerked it from its loops. He put the buckle in his palm and twisted the leather around his hand until about two feet of strap dangled free. "Git over here." He raised the belt over his head, the free end hung down behind him.

Just as he tried to swing the leather toward the young woman, Shayla caught the loose end. "I don't think so, Mister."

The man turned in his tracks. "Where'd you gals come from?" He blinked, then said, "Heck, it don't matter, I'll beat the tar outta all three of you'ens, then I'll see how fur my stamina 'll take me." He laughed a sickening snicker. "This could be fun."

Ressa shouted, "Why are you going to beat her?"

"Cuz it makes the makin-up more fun."

Shayla's face twisted. "You're a sick man."

He laughed again. "Ya don't say?" and he started toward her. "Come here, little missy and gives me a smooch."

Shayla put her hand out in front of her. "You will not touch me, in Jesus' name."

"Don't you 'Jesus' me you little missionary. I don't talk to him or listen to him."

"Well, you'll listen to me now and you'll not touch me or either of these two girls. God has given his angels charge over me and will keep me in all of my ways."[xii]

The man lifted his hand in front of her face. "This belt'll knock you off your high horse, Miss Priss."

Shayla didn't blink, but mumbled, "Abba, give me wisdom!" She crossed her wrists high above her head and shouted. "No weapon formed against me will prosper!"[xiii] She propelled her hands down and apart in front of her and spread her arms to the sides with her fists balled into knots.

The man chuckled. "Girly, is that supposed to sker me?" He laughed and tried to move toward her.

"If you try to touch me, you will feel your hands go weak and you will drop that belt. Your arms will go limp at your sides and they will start to tingle. If you persist in trying to move toward me, your mouth will go dry and you will lose control of your bladder and wet yourself."

A hideous *he-he-he* escaped from his lips. "You are just downright entertainin, darlin." And he stepped toward her. The belt began to uncoil, as his hand went limp. His eyes flew open wide. He tried to grab the belt with his other hand, but both arms flapped useless at his sides. "What are you, some kinda witch or somethin?" He tried to step again and began to cough and spit. All of a sudden, he lost control of his bladder and a puddle of yellow liquid formed on the floor around his feet.

Shayla's head tilted toward the man. "Now do you believe me? You are going to stand here until you repent before the Lord. You will not leave this room the same as you came in. We are going to leave now and you will never look for us, do you understand me?"

His head bobbed up and down, his wide eyes stared at her.

Shayla took Ressa by the hand and led her toward the door, she looked at the other girl who stood speechless. "Are you coming with us?"

The girl nodded in silence.

Shayla turned the doorknob and came face to face with a man who must have been the girl's pimp.

"I heard yellin, Carla, what's goin on in there?"

Shayla stared into his eyes and pulled the door open wide. She pointed behind her. "Do you see that man?" She glanced at him. "If you try to follow us or try to sell Carla again, you are going to end up just like him. Do you understand me?"

Before Shayla saw it coming, he had drawn back and when she turned to face the man again, the back of his hand slapped her across the face.

Carla sprang at him, grabbed his beard and pulled her knee up between his legs as hard as she could. He crumpled to the floor. "You don't hit girls any more, do you hear me?"

He shook his head from his place on the floor.

Doors began to open up and down the hall. Carla yelled, "Girls, we are out of here. We don't work for him anymore."

Shayla shouted, "Anyone who wants to be free and have a new life, come with us." She headed toward the stairs, followed by Ressa and other girls of all ages.

A man pulling up his trousers stepped out of a room and tried to stop them.

With one quick stroke, Shayla shoved the heel of her hand up under his chin. His head flew back, hit the wall and he slid to the floor. A couple of girls spat on him as they walked by.

They exited the grungy hotel and were met at the curb by a van with the words *Abba's House* written on the side. Shayla approached the driver and asked, "Who sent you?"

The man patted the side of the van. "Like it says, lady, Abba's House."

"I will take your tag number, mister, and if anything happens to these girls ..."

He stuck out his hand and gave her a card. "The number is already written there for you and my name with my picture is on the other side."

Shayla glanced at the picture and back at his face. She turned to the line of girls behind her. "Ladies, your ride is here."

When all of the girls except Carla, Shayla and Ressa were settled in the van, Shayla turned, "Carla, aren't you going with them?"

"Nah, I have an appointment for an abortion. I need to get there."

Shayla waved her hands. "No, don't please. Let me find you some help."

She stuck one hand on her hip. "I don't need no help, girlfriend, I just need to get rid of this baby."

With eyes closed, Shayla whispered, "Father, what do I say?" A warm calm came over her. "Carla, God says, if you will trust Him and let this baby live, it will be the best thing that has ever happened to you. Will you trust Him?"

She thought for a moment and said, "What if you're wrong?"

The driver leaned out his window. "She's not

wrong, Carla. Get in, we'll take care of you and find a wonderful family for this baby."

Carla reluctantly crawled in and closed the door. "You'd better be right girl, or I'll come looking for you."

The driver laughed and looked at Shayla. "You are to go to the cafe at the end of the street. A man with a bird wants to see you." The van eased away from the curb and roared away, down the street.

As the girls strolled toward the restaurant, Ressa looked up at her. "I've never seen you hit anyone before."

"I know, it surprised me too, but I heard 'danger,' and before I knew it, the heel of my hand was up under his chin. Then the scriptures came to me that David was a warrior,[xiv] but he was also a man after God's own heart.[xv] He also asked the Lord to teach his hands to war and his fingers to fight.[xvi] Then I remembered that Jesus' disciples carried swords.[xvii] I guess it depends on how God's Spirit is leading you. I've never had to fight before, I've always used God's word and my faith, but it seems that the battle is getting more difficult." She touched the side of her face where it still stung from the slap. "We can only trust in the Lord and lean on his Spirit, not on our own understanding.[xviii]

They reached the cafe and pushed the door open, the place was deserted except for the waitress behind the counter.

"Can I help, you two?"

Shayla glanced around, but said, "We're supposed to meet a man here. I guess we're early."

The lady smiled. "Would that be a man with a bird?"

Shayla stared at her. "Yes, it would."

The waitress tipped her head toward the back corner of the restaurant.

Shayla and Ressa walked, as if in a dream, when they arrived at the corner, there was a poster of a pirate with a parrot on his shoulder. She glanced back to the waitress.

"Lean not on your own understanding, sugar. Go on now."

Chapter 8

Shanghaied

To keep from banging her nose against the wall, Shayla stuck one hand out in front of her face, but the poster gave way and she stepped onto a street corner, pulling Ressa through with her.

Ressa looked around. "Where do you think we are now?"

"I don't know yet, little one."

A big blue car rolled up to the curb. A very handsome, friendly man spoke to them through the open window. "Are you girls working or are you lost?" and he chuckled.

"We're sort of lost," said Shayla, "can you tell us where we are?"

"You're at the corner of New Amsterdam and Tenth Street."

Shayla lifted one hand, palm up. "No, I mean, what city are we in?"

The man whistled. "You two are lost. This is the worst end of Bay Town that you could be in. How'd you get here?"

Ressa lifted her shoulders and her palm turned up too. "That's a very long story, mister."

"Call me, Gregory. Do you need a lift somewhere?" He stepped from his car.

Shayla glanced up and down the street. "Well, we don't really know where to go."

Gregory motioned toward the back of his car. "I have a map back here, let's see if that would help." He used a clicker to open his trunk and Shayla followed him.

Ressa yanked Shayla's arm and whined, "No, Shay."

When Shayla looked back at her, Gregory grabbed them both. He lifted Ressa by one arm shoving her into the trunk, then he pushed Shayla in on top of her and slammed it shut.

Shayla scooted over to give Ressa room. "Are you okay? That didn't go so well, did it?"

"Didn't you hear the bird's warning?"

"No, I'm afraid I didn't. Good thing I had you to warn me, little one."

Ressa grabbed her hand. "That's not funny, Shay. I warned you too late, I thought you knew he was bad. We need to pray." And for the first time, Ressa led in prayer. "Abba, I believe that you sent us through that poster, but why did we get snatched by Mr. Cheesy Not-So-Nice Guy? And how do we get out?"

Shayla whispered, "That's weird, I thought I heard him say to stay where we are."

Ressa rolled toward her. "Me too, I thought I was going, you know, whacko, or something."

The car bumped across railroad tracks at a high speed. Both girls hit their heads on the inside of the trunk lid.

Shayla rubbed her bump. "Ouch! Abba what's up with this?"

The Spirit whispered, "Shanghaied?"

Then she told Ressa, "We're being Shanghaied." But she clarified. "Oh, some other kids are being Shanghaied. Got it, Abba."

Ressa twisted beside her. "What does Shang-whatever mean?"

"It's a term I've heard on television or in movies. It usually means to force people onto a ship to work as slaves. I guess we are being taken to a group of people who are being …"

The car screeched to a stop, the car door opened and they heard Gregory's voice. "Help me over here. I have two more for the store."

Shayla whispered, "We're going to a store."

The clicker beeped and the trunk lid sprung open. Bright light and salty sea air greeted them.

One man reached in and scooped Shayla up, but tore her dress on the trunk latch as he pulled her out.

Gregory yelled at him. "Don't damage the merchandise, idiot."

The man plopped Shayla down hard on her feet.

"Ow, you baboon."

The man drew his hand back to smack her, but Gregory stopped him. "I said, don't damage the merch."

Gregory reached in and took Ressa's hand. "Do you need some help getting out?

"Yeah, but you bruised my arm putting me in there." When her feet landed, she pulled her hand away and rubbed her throbbing arm.

The girls peered around and they were at a seaport. A large ship bobbed in the water behind a group of girls and boys of all ages standing in a huddle beside a big platform. A group of men, some well-dressed, some scuzzy-looking, stood near-by.

Gregory grabbed each of them by an arm, led them to the group of kids and shoved them into the pack, then jumped onto the platform. The man who had scooped Shayla out of the trunk picked up a little boy of maybe six-years of age and stood him on the front of stage. "Gentlemen, what is my bid on this fine lad?"

Shayla gasped. "Shanghaied!" She whispered, "These kids are being sold."

Ressa whispered back, "You mean, *we're* being sold. What do we do?"

Shayla looked at the ground. "Abba, Abba,

where are you?"

The invisible pressure of the dove lit on her shoulder.

She stared at the ground and asked, "What do we do?"

Words drifted into her mind. "Calm down and don't draw attention to yourself. Now quietly spread the word, 'Get ready to mutiny' to the children. Let me handle the rest."

Shayla bent close to her friend's ear. "Ressa, whisper the words 'Get ready to mutiny' to the girl in front of you and tell her to pass it on."

She obeyed without hesitation. The girl in front of her did the same.

Gregory's voice bellowed. "A hundred dollars? Men, look at this face." He tilted the boy's chin up toward the crowd. "Think how many times you can get a hundred dollars for a night with this boy."

A man in the front shouted, "Two hundred!"

A hand flew up from a man on the other side of the group. "Three hundred!"

From the back, a powerful voice yelled, "A thousand dollars!"

Gregory tiptoed to see the bidder. "Sold, to the man with good taste." He pointed to his partner who pulled the boy from the stage and put a young girl in his place. Gregory whispered to the brute, "Go collect the money, then deliver the boy."

Gregory glanced at the delicate girl. "What's my

bid for this porcelain doll?

A man shouted from the center of the pack. "Five hundred."

"Any other bids? Look at this child." A similar lifting of her head presented her face to the crowd. "She's pretty now, but she'll be a beauty one day."

"Six hundred!"

"Six hundred, only six hundred? Men! What's the problem?"

"One man shouted, I'm waiting for that curly-headed one in the blue dress."

Shayla's face flashed hot.

The crowd howled with laughter.

"Patience, men. Little ones first."

Gregory yelled, "Six hundred once, six hundred twice. Sold."

Gregory's brute reached for the little girl.

The buyer shouted, "Don't bruise her."

The crowd got restless, a man shouted, "Get to the big girl."

Another bellowed in agreement. "Yeah, curly-top!"

Still another shouted, "Put her on the platform."

Gregory tried to calm the crowd. "Gentlemen! Please!" He exhaled a long breath. "Okay, you win. Kyle, get the new girl in the blue dress."

Kyle reached for Shayla and lifted her out of the group of children like someone would pick a flower.

Before she knew it, she had been plopped onto the platform to stand in front of the crowd of men.

One man shouted, "She has a bruise on her cheekbone."

Shayla raised her hand and cradled the spot where Carla's pimp had hit her.

"She'll mend, it's only a light bruise and it was there when I got her. What's my bid?"

"A thousand," yelled a man on the left.

"Six thousand," shouted a man in the back.

Shayla turned to the side and saw Gregory grin. "That's more like it, boys. Do I hear seven?"

"Twenty thousand!" shouted a man in the middle.

A roar went up from the crowd.

The man in the back shouted, "You knew I wanted her!"

"Then outbid me, you miserable wimp."

A different man yelled, "Twenty-two thousand."

The man who was being outbid screamed, "You jerk! You're just trying to steal what I want."

Shayla heard in her ear. "Mutiny now." She turned to Ressa and mouthed the words, "Mutiny now."

Ressa poked the girl in front of her and whispered, "Mutiny now."

The girl screamed, "Mutiny! Go! Now!"

Thirty or so kids began to scatter from the platform.

The man who bid twenty-two thousand yelled profanity at the man who was angry.

The man in the back tried to push through the crowd of men, knocking some to the ground. They scrambled to their feet and retaliated. The man to the left laughed, another man punched him in the face. A full-scale brawl broke out.

Children ran in every direction.

Suddenly, the blare of sirens filled the air. Blue lights reflected off of every hard surface as police cars skidded into the area. Gregory tried to run, but Shayla's foot found his ankle and he sailed from the platform, face first.

Two policemen scooped him from the pavement. One looked up at Shayla and asked, "Are you okay, Miss?"

"I am now. How did you know to come here?"

"An old guy with a bird told us there was a mob fight going on. Do you need help getting down?"

"Yes, thank you and I need to find my friend, Ressa."

A familiar voice shouted from the chaos. "Here I am, Shay."

"Thank goodness, you're all right." She turned to the policeman. "Officer, all of these children were being sold to those men who are fighting. Will you call someone to help them find their parents?"

"Sure, but what about you and your friend?"

Shayla grinned. "The old gentleman with the

bird will be along any minute to get us, but thank you for all of your help."

"Yes, ma'am, we'll get all of these buyers and the seller in cuffs, Social Services has already been contacted. We'll take care of the children until their parents are located." He smiled and turned. With his hand on the cuffs around Gregory's wrists he shoved him toward his squad car.

Ressa looked up at her friend. "What do we do now, Shay?"

"We pray."

When the prayer ended, a piece of paper with an arrow drawn on it floated to their feet.

Ressa lifted her shoulders. "I guess we go that way," and pointed the direction of the arrow.

Two blocks from the waterfront, they came face-to-face with a picture of two girls, one with straight hair, one with curls. Above the figures a sign read, *Enter Here!*

Shayla reached for Ressa's hand. "I guess we go in, little one." She smiled at her friend, but Shayla's nose bent sideways as she pressed against the paper, then she and Ressa popped through into a room full of teenagers. Loud music blared in their ears. One guy stepped forward and handed each girl a drink.

"No, thank you!" Shayla shouted.

The teen boy yelled back, "What's wrong, you too good to share a drink with me?"

"No, I don't drink alcohol, that's all."

"Why didn't you say so, come over to the table, we've got lots of options."

She reluctantly followed him. "Here you go, girls, we've got chips too."

Ressa reached for a handful of potato chips.

Shayla poured them some cola.

Ressa's eyes searched the room before she shouted, "Why do you think we're here, Shay?"

Chapter 9

Separated

Shayla bent close to Ressa's ear. "I'm not sure, but we need to wait a bit to see if we get any instructions from Abba."

A voice behind her laughed. "How old are you, my grandmother talks about a band called Abba?"

Ressa shouted over the thumping of the music. "No, Abba's the King."

The girl laughed again. "My grandmother says Elvis was the King."

Ressa tried to explain, but Shayla pointed out that the girl had been drinking and wasn't coherent enough to understand.

They sat down and offered the girl a chair next to them, but she refused and wandered off.

Moments later Ressa tapped Shayla on the shoulder. "Look, those guys are taking that girl out the backdoor."

Shayla jumped up and pushed her way through the dancing teens, reaching the door as the two men pushed the girl into a van. She dashed out, followed by Ressa. "Stop it! Let her go!"

The driver jumped from the idling van and hooked his arm around Shayla's waist. "Here's another one."

Ressa flailed her arms and shouted. "No, don't take her!" but Shayla was shoved in and the van door slid shut.

The driver hopped behind the wheel. With his arm out the window, he pushed Ressa back and shouted, "Scram, nugget, or we'll pack you in too."

She dashed toward the side door of the van and pulled the handle, but it was locked.

Shayla's hands pressed against the window as the vehicle sped away, knocking her friend to the ground. "Abba, what are we going to do? Be with Ressa, protect her and guide her. Give me wisdom and direction, in Jesus' name. Amen."

The van plunged through the dark streets, an occasional light flickered past the window. Seconds turned into minutes, minutes into hours. Where were they taking her? The drunken girl lay on the floor and vomited in the back of the van. The smell engulfed Shayla, fear gripped her, when all of a sudden, she heard a whisper in her ear. "Fear not, Ressa is safe and you will be safe too, I am with you." Shayla's body relaxed and she leaned against a wheel well, the swaying of the van eventually rocked her to sleep.

The sun rose and peeked through the windows of the motionless van. The girl in the rear, belched, groaned and sat up. "Where are we?"

"I don't know, they've driven us here through the night."

"You must be joking. It's one of my friends pranking us."

Shayla leaned toward her. "I'm not joking and we are in serious trouble. You were so drunk, you didn't even resist the two guys who grabbed you."

The girl sneered at her. "So, what are you doing here if you weren't drunk?"

Shayla avoided eye contact with her. "I tried to help you and they pushed me in here too. My younger friend got left behind."

The girl rose to her knees and pushed her hair from her face. "You're serious about all of this?"

"Yes."

The girl plopped down crossed-legged. "What are we going to do?"

Shayla lifted her eyes. "What's your name?"

"I'm Sharrin. Sharrin Sanders."

"We need to pray, Sharrin."

The girls scoffed. "We need to what? I've never prayed in my life."

"Don't you think now would be a good time to start? I believe God sent me here to help you."

"God sent you—to help me? Then why are you in here with me?" and she laughed.

"I couldn't very well have helped you if they hadn't taken me, now could I?"

Sharrin leaned forward. "Well, duh, you could have gotten the tag number of the van, the color, a description of the men, dummy."

Shayla looked down. "And you would have been here all alone."

Sharrin pushed back. "Yeah, but what good are you in here? Huh?"

With eyes closed, Shayla prayed. "Heavenly Father, you have been so good to me, I'm trusting you to show me what to do and how to get Sharrin and myself out of this mess."

The girl folded her arms. "A lotta good that's going to do."

Instantly the van door slid open. A man reached in and grabbed Sharrin. She struggled against him, but he stuck a small instrument in her side. With a crackle and a gasp, Sharrin fell limp.

"That'll shut her up for a while."

A woman stepped forward. "She stinks. Take her to the bathroom and lock her in." She turned toward Shayla. "Are we going to have to taser you too?" She gave a sarcastic grin. "At least you don't reek of alcohol and vomit like your friend, but you do look a little worse for wear." She glanced back at a waiting thug. "Take her to the bathroom too. Lock them both in, I'll get them some fresh clothes."

The man grasped Shayla by the wrist. "Come on."

Shayla blurted out from behind him. "Don't bruise me, the customers won't like that. They like to do the bruising themselves."

His wide eyes, flashed back toward her. "I see you are familiar with the pleasure industry." His brown stained teeth showed between his snarled lips.

She bellowed back. "I've never found it to be a pleasure personally. How would you like for your daughter or sister to be involved in this?"

He tossed his head back and laughed. "You just met my sister Sable, why don't you ask her when she brings you your clothes."

With a snarky grin, Shayla said, "Your parents must be so proud!"

He dragged her into the house, then wheeled around and the back of his hand caught Shayla across the mouth. "Now look what you made me do. I probably won't get any dessert tonight if your lip swells." He showed his ugly teeth again and pushed her into the bathroom.

Sharrin lunged at her. "What are we going to do?"

Grabbing her by the shoulders, Shayla replied,

"We are going to calm down and get cleaned up. Do you want to shower first?"

The door opened and the woman stepped in with fresh clothes and underwear. "There is shampoo and soap in the shower. Now move it!"

Shayla sweetened her voice and face. "Thank you, may I ask if we can get something to eat? It's been a while since we've had any real food."

A sour look crossed her face. "If, if mind you, if I see that you are cooperating, I will have something for you when you are cleaned up and dressed. Shower, wash your hair too and dry it, before you knock on this door." She pointed behind her, then turned, walked out and locked it.

Sharrin folded her arms, "Well, she can just go where the sun don't shine if she thinks I'm going to cooperate."

"Look at yourself in the mirror."

She turned Sharrin to face the glass.

The girl snarled at the vomit dried in her hair and crusted onto her cheek.

An encouraging word came from Shayla. "Don't you at least want to bathe and put on clean clothes?"

"What's your name, Miss Persnickety?"

"I'm Shayla, but you can call me Shay."

Sharrin's face grew serious and drawn. "What do you think they are going to do with us?"

Shayla turned her around. "Why don't you get

in the shower and I'll tell you what I can."

The water came on and Shayla proceeded to share as much information with Sharrin as she could.

"Do you think we are going to stay here in this house or do you think they are going to move us? Do you think they will try to sell us, like you said that guy Gregory did?"

"Sorry, Sharrin, it's too soon to know. I've seen all types of places from plush to shabby and then there were those men down at the dock. We'll have to pretend to play along until we figure out where we are and what to do."

Even without seeing her face, Shayla could tell from her voice that Sharrin's eyebrows arched up.

"How far do we have to go to play along?"

"I mean, like getting cleaned up and dressed. I don't intend to let any man touch me in an indecent way, or you either if I can help it, but we need to be ready to fight and we need to pray."

Over the noise of the shower, Sharrin shouted. "What good is praying going to do?"

Shayla folded her arms and rested against the sink. "Prayer's a powerful weapon if you are praying to the right person."

A snarky voice rose about the sound of the water. "Like which god do you pray to?"

Shayla smiled. "I pray to the one true God, and His Son Jesus, the Ones who've rescued me so many times I've lost count and who have loved me even when I've messed up. I love them and trust them. They sent me on this mission and I believe they'll guide me."

"If He's so great, why did he send me on this mission too?" The door cracked open.

Shayla looked at her with stern eyes. "He didn't send you on this mission, Sharrin, you wouldn't listen to me and you got yourself into this because you were reckless. You're not on a mission because you *are* the mission. Now dry your hair and let me shower."

Moments later, Shayla had showered and was drying her hair when Sharrin asked, "Am I really the mission? Did I get you into this?"

"Yes, that's true, you are the mission, but I'm sorry I was so sharp with you. I believe, no, I know that God led me to that party and He placed you in my path. When I saw those two guys dragging you out of there, I had to do something, but I wish I hadn't gotten separated from my friend Ressa. She's only twelve."

Sharrin ducked her chin. "How old to you think I am?"

"Probably sixteen or seventeen, about my age."

Tears leaked down Sharrin's cheeks. "I'm only thirteen."

Shayla straightened abruptly. "You're what?

With all of that makeup and your poofed-up hair, you looked so much older."

"I know, I was trying to prove I was like the other girls and I thought drinking would be fun and sophisticated, but I didn't look so sophisticated with puke on my face and in my hair, did I?" She wept.

Shayla patted her on the shoulder. "Look, I don't know how yet, but I'm going to try to get you back to the party and try to find Ressa."

She jerked her tear stained face up. "I don't want to go back to the party. Please, don't make me."

"Okay, chill, but I need to find Ressa."

The door swung open with force, Sable marched into the room. "Are you two going to stay in here all day? Let me look at you." Her eyes scanned the girls. "What are you waiting on? Get your clothes on."

Shayla held a knit dress up in front of her. "I think this is too small for me."

A cruel laugh escaped from Sable's twisted lips. "The men are going to like it, now get dressed." She slammed the door behind her again.

The girls wriggled into the small dresses and faced the mirror.

"This is embarrassing," said Shayla.

"There was a time when I would've thought you looked just right." Sharrin lowered her eyes toward the floor. "But now I see the danger in playing games like that. I'm so sorry Shay."

"As long as you see the problem, that's part of the solution," replied Shayla. "Now how are we going to get out of here?"

The door flung inward again. "Okay, cupcakes, let's get some frosting on you." Sable entered with a makeup case. "Let's see now. You, curly-head, come over here. I think this eye shadow will look great with that black dress. Sit down." Sable grabbed her by the shoulder and plunked Shayla down on a stool. "Look up at the light, now close your eyes."

When Sable had finished and moved out of the way, Shayla saw her own reflection in the mirror, but it wasn't her. That hussy couldn't be her. "What have you done to me?"

"I've made you presentable to our clientele. This is just the way they like 'em."

Then it was Sharrin's turn on the stool.

She turned out looking much like she did when Shayla first met her.

Sable pointed. "Out the door with you."

They were led downstairs to a big room. Other girls already sat on grungy, crushed velvet chairs scattered throughout the parlor. A fireplace with a mantel and mirror anchored one end, the opposite side harbored the front door. Sable flipped on some country music and turned toward the girls. "Smile girls, we're open for business."

With eyes squeezed tight, Shayla prayed, "Father, I trust you, but this place is frightening. Show me how to get myself and Sharrin out of here and what about these other girls, Father, what am I to do?"

The girl next to her leaned over and whispered, "You'd better get rid of your pet bird, before Sable sees him, she might eat him." She twisted her mouth. "Or is he part of your routine?"

Shayla turned to the stranger. "How did you get into this mess?"

The girl replied. "My step-daddy and his brother use to take it for free, so I swore that when I was old enough, anybody else who touched me would pay for it."

Shayla bristled. "That's awful. Did you try to tell anybody?"

"Yeah, I told my momma and she said she'd tear me up if I kept lying, so I left. That was three years ago."

"That's terrible, I'm sorry she wouldn't believe you, but … " Suddenly, a wave of calm filled Shayla's spirit and she looked up. "I'm waiting on you, Father."

The door squeaked open. Two urban cowboys strode into the room.

Sable greeted them. "Hiya boys, what's your names?"

"Hello, I'm Beau and this here's my friend,

Norton."

Sable grinned. "I haven't seen you two here before. Who recommended my little dining establishment?"

"Ah, ma'am, there ain't hardly a man on the off-shore rigs that hasn't talked about your place. They say we can get a fine dinner," he winked, "and a tasty dessert."

"You boys flatter me beyond words. Here's the menu." She swept her hand across the room. "Look around and take your pick. If you want anything special, all you gotta do is ask."

Norton took off his hat and held it in front of him. "We know, ma'am, but is there any new blood this week?"

She pointed in Shayla and Sharrin's direction.

He and Beau strolled their way.

Beau also took off his hat. "Hi-dee, ladies. I'm Beau, me and my friend have been working off-shore all week and we sure would like some company. We haven't had any super yet, would you like to join us?"

Sharrin turned her face away and said, "No thanks!"

But Shayla said, "I'm starved. They haven't fed us since they kidnapped us and brought us here."

Sharrin spun toward Shayla.

Beau laughed, "Kidnapped you, golly miss, isn't that a little dramatic?"

She leaned forward. "No Beau, it isn't. They pushed Sharrin," she pointed at the girl, "into a van and I tried to stop them so they flung me in too. Look at my cheek, this is where one pimp popped me for trying to rescue his girl. And see my lip puffing up? Sable's brother did that to me this morning. I would love it if you could get us some food."

All of the girls around the room stared at her.

"Gee, miss, I'd be honored to buy you and your friend some dinner." He looked at Sable. "We'll have dinner with these girls, take us to your dining room."

Sable frowned at Shayla as she passed. "This way, gentlemen—and ladies." She opened the door to the stairs and led the way, at the top, she pointed toward two doors. "Which of you would like the Rodeo Room?"

Beau stepped forward and looked inside the first room. A big poster bed sat in the middle of a room decorated with western décor. "What's in the other room?"

"It's painted like a saloon." Sable grinned. "We call this one the Tall Order Room. Which of you would like a stiff drink?" She turned to the men.

Norton asked, "So when are we served our meals?"

Sable tossed her head back and laughed. "Are you serious, cowboy? This ain't no restaurant. Tarts are all we serve here."

Norton reached into his inside coat pocket and pulled out a Marshal's badge. "Then I'm afraid you are under arrest, for solicitation and if this young lady is telling the truth, we're going to add kidnapping and unlawful imprisonment to the charge."

Sharrin flashed a look at Shayla who said, "And add child endangerment to the list, this girl is only thirteen-years-old."

Norton pulled Sable's hands behind her and cuffed her.

Beau lifted his arm and spoke into his sleeve. "Okay men, come in and clear this place." He looked at Shayla. "What's your name, miss?"

"I'm Shayla McKnight from Sallis, Tennessee."

Beau whistled. "Wow, you're a long way from home."

"Were you serious about those accusations, Shayla?"

"She sure was, officer," shouted Sharrin.

"It's Deputy, miss, he pulled a card from his pocket and handed it to Sharrin."

Shayla saw the number, 361-555-7777.

He continued, "And you'll both need to come along with us and give a statement."

Shayla turned to him. "First, I need to find my friend, Teressa. We were together when Sable's brother and another guy grabbed Sharrin last night at a party, they grabbed me too, but left Teressa."

"Where was the party?" asked Norton.

Stumped for an answer, Shayla shrugged her shoulders. "I don't know?"

"If you don't have the exact address, just give us the street and city."

Sharrin jumped to her rescue. "It was in Morgan City, Arkansas. They drove us all night to get here."

Beau scratched his chin. "That's across state lines, you're on the gulf coast of Texas now. We'll have to up Sable's charges to federal trafficking and get the FBI involved. This has been a pretty good day for us, but I'm sorry for the troubles you girls have had."

Shayla closed her eyes and whispered, "But how am I going to get back to Ressa?"

Pointing to the end of the hall, Sharrin said, "Why don't you ask that man over there, the one with the bird on his shoulder. He's motioning for you to come to him."

When Shayla opened her eyes, all she saw at the end of the hall was a full-length mirror. "Where is he?"

Sharrin scrunched up her face and pointed again. "Standing right down there, dummy."

When Shayla walked down the hallway, Sharrin's mouth flew open as Shayla walked straight through the man, but stopped just before the mirror and turned to face her.

Beau turned around. "Where's your friend?"

"She, uh, she … there was this old man with a bird at the end of the hall …. You're going to think I've been drugged …"

Beau stared at her. "Just tell me, miss."

"The old man was waving for Shay to come and she walked right through him."

Beau folded one arm across his chest and propped the other elbow on top of that hand. He whispered into his fist. "Abba!"

Sharrin had had enough, she flapped her arms out to her side and yelled, "Who is this guy?"

The Deputy leaned toward her and said, "I tell you what, I'll ride back in the van with you girls and explain everything. I especially want to tell you about Abba's Son and what He did for you."

"Is he the guy who tipped you off to this place?"

Beau grinned and lifted his hand to gesture toward the stairs. "This way, please."

As Beau and Sharrin entered the stairway, Shayla turned and vanished into the mirror.

Chapter 10

Whirling and Tossing

Shayla bounced into a messy room, clothes all over the floor, a radio blaring and a young girl, about Ressa's age, bent over a laptop.

She heard a noise behind her and jerked around to face Shayla. "Who the blazes are you? Someone my mom sent to spy on me?"

Stepping forward, Shayla tried to defend herself, but what could she say? "I'm Shayla, I've come to … ."

"Stop it right there, spy. I'm getting' outta here, so get out of my face." The girl rose from the computer and dashed to the window.

"But where're you going? And what's your name?"

"If my mom hired you, spy, you'd know my name and if she didn't, what the heck're you doing in my room? Now leave me alone."

Shayla stepped in front of her. "But I'm here

to," her voice trailed off, "rescue you."

The girl reached the window, unlocked it and pushed it open. "Lying, spy, devil-dog. Move!" Stepping onto a stool she lifted herself to the window sill and sat down. "I'm going to meet the love of my life, the only person who understands me, now like I said, leave me alone."

Reaching her hands forward, Shayla yelled, "Wait, who is this person?"

"He's number 5LuvGuru."

Wide-eyed Shayla shouted, "What? You don't even know his real name?"

"His name isn't important. He knows me, he understands me and he loves me for who I am." Her legs swung through the window and she leapt into the front yard."

Bristling, Shayla growled, "Grrrr, wait for me, girl." Shayla climbed through the window and dropped onto the grass, but the girl was fast and had a lead. They raced down the sidewalk to a main street. The girl caught a break with the light, but Shayla had to wait. Across the street at a bus stop, Shayla saw a man lurking. The girl stood under the clear shelter and looked back and forth. The man stepped toward her and grabbed her arm. The traffic light changed.

Shayla dashed across and ran to the girl, but the man shoved her into a waiting car. Shayla reached them and tried to push the man away, but he was large and strong. He grabbed Shayla and pushed her into the backseat too, then slammed the door. There was no door handle inside and a wire screen isolated them from the front seat. The man climbed in and the driver sped away.

The frightened girl clung to Shayla's arm. "How'd you know I needed to be rescued? Did you set this up?"

Shaking her head, Shayla protested. "No! I didn't set this up, but …" she stammered, "your daddy knew you were in trouble."

"My daddy? He ain't been around for a long time! And who are you, in your slinky, black, hooker outfit?"

Shayla looked down at her tight knit dress. "I'm undercover and this is my disguise." She leaned close. "These men have been luring kids to meet them and then … ."

"Then what?"

"We'll have to wait to see."

Moments later they pulled into an underground garage and parked. The brute jerked the door open. "Git out!"

Shayla slid to the door and tugged at the hem of her dress.

The man tossed his head back and laughed. "I see someone's already dressed for work. That was considerate of you. Come on, now git out."

Shayla stared into his face. "You won't get away with this. There is a day of reckoning coming.[xix]

"Yeah, yeah, shut up, bimbo." He grabbed her by the arm and yanked her from the car. "Next! Come on out, SweetCheeks13."

The girl's face appeared at the opening. "How'd you know my screen name? Did Guru tell you? Is he here?"

The two men now stood together. The bigger one laughed and winked at the one who had driven. "Well, *my darling dream girl. Can't wait to meet IRL.*" Both burst out laughing. "Now maybe we can do some of that *in real life* sexy stuff we've been chattin' about."

She snatched her hands over her mouth and squealed.

The driver grabbed her and jerked her to her feet. "Come on Sweet Cheeks, let's get this party started."

The girl and Shayla were forced into an elevator. The big man sighed. "Next stop, *heaven.*" And laughed again.

Shayla whispered, "What's your name?"

The girl, still smart mouthed replied, "Shouldn't you know who you are rescuing? Huh?"

Shayla pursed her lips together then replied, "Yes, I should, so tell me your name, Sweet Cheeks."

The girl glared at her. "I'm Amber, what was

your dumb name? Sperla, or something."

"I see you're not going to make this easy. I'm Shayla, but you can call me Shay."

The girl glared at her. "So very nice to meet you, Spy."

"Look Amber, I'm trying … "

The elevator stopped. The door slid open. A penthouse apartment came into view.

The men in front of them stepped aside. "Welcome to your new digs, tramps."

Across the room, a man stood, floor to ceiling windows revealed the city skyline behind him. "Now Buster, that's no way to talk to our guests. And I see there are no new boys this time? I am disappointed."

Amber rushed forward. "Are you Guru?"

The man spread his arms wide. "Darling, we are all love gurus." He gestured with both hands. "Please come to me."

Amber backed away, but bumped into Buster. His gruff voice rolled out behind her. "Girlies, this is the man who knows your hearts' desires. This is Allister. You've wanted to meet him, Sweet Cheeks," his voice changed. "Now git over there!" And he shoved Amber from behind.

Allister strolled forward and sashayed around Amber. "She needs some work, but the black-dressed girl is fine. Put them with the others, our guests will be here shortly. See that the girls are ready."

Buster grabbed Shayla and Amber by the arm, forcing them down the hallway and into a room with several other girls.

When the door closed, Shayla stepped forward. "Girls, listen to me." Heads turned her direction. "I'm here to rescue you."

Amber laughed. "Yeah right, but you're in here with us."

Shayla pursed her lips again. "I know it looks that way, but I need to know something. How many of you ended up here because you were lured here on your computers?"

Most of the hands went up.

"Girls don't you know how dangerous that is?"

Amber folded her arms across her body and leaned to one side. "Well, duh, Sperla. Knowing how we got in here doesn't help to get us out."

Shayla looked at the floor. "I know, but now I need you all to trust me and do what I say. How many of you know Abba?"

One hand went up.

Shayla continued. "Okay, Abba forgives you for getting into this mess, now I need for you to pray for him to give me wisdom."

The girl nodded and closed her eyes.

Shayla felt a flutter near her ear. "Okay, girls do any of you know where the emergency stairs are?"

A couple of girls nodded and one said, "But the

door is locked."

"That's okay, when they come to get us, I'll take the lead. I'll struggle to distract Buster," she pointed, "I want you two to lead the other girls to the stairway, it will be unlocked this time."

One girl asked, "What about you?"

"Don't worry about me, I'll be okay. Got it?"

All of the girls nodded.

The door behind her opened and Shayla prepared to fight, but clothes were thrown in at her instead. "Give those to Sweet Cheeks." Buster cackled.

She held them up.

Amber looked at them and said, "Oooo, those are cute."

Shayla frowned. "No, they aren't, you'd look like a hoochie momma in these."

"You're a fine one to talk. You look like you're wearing a plastic tube."

She hung her head. "I know, but at the last place, they made me put this on and I haven't had time to change."

Amber spread her hands. "So, you've been in another place like this? How'd you get out?"

Her shoulders rose. "That's a long story, but I need for you to trust me for now. Will you do that?"

"One of the young girls piped in. "I will!"

Other girls shouted and nodded. "We will too."

The door opened again. Buster's voice broke

through the shouts. "Shut up, all of ya! Line up and follow me."

Shayla stepped into the hall and walked forward. Several feet from the door of the room, she spread her feet and her arms to reach the walls and braced herself.

Buster came up behind her and pushed on her shoulders, but she didn't budge. "That's not possible." He shoved her again, but nothing. He tried to pull her arms down. Nothing.

Girls behind them slipped out of the room and crept to the door at the end of the hall. True to Shayla's word, it was unlocked, but as it cracked open, an alarm blared. The girls panicked and scrambled through the door and dashed down the stairs.

Buster turned and ran toward them. Shayla whirled around and threw her arms around his neck and tried to pull him back, but he was too strong. She wrestled him as best she could, but he flung her to the floor.

Allister appeared in the entryway of the hall. "What the devil is going on here?"

Buster charged at the exit door, but it slammed shut and locked behind the last girl. He spun toward Shayla who was lifting herself from the floor. He pointed. "This tramp helped the others escape."

Allister fluttered forward. "That can't be true. Check the room, the gents are here."

Buster gripped Shayla's arm, peered into the empty room and yelled. "This here's the only one left." He glared at her. "I guess we'll have to spread her around," and he snickered.

Allister turned and shuffled to the living room followed by Buster with Shayla in his grasp.

Having heard the alarm, several men had returned to the elevator and frantically pushed the button.

"Gentlemen, gentlemen, no need to panic." He placed one hand on his hip and one hand tipped calmly in the air. "True, we've had a small set-back, but we will proceed with hors d'oeuvres and champagne. I'm sure all will work itself out."

At that moment the elevator bell dinged. The men standing in front of it turned to enter. As the doors slid apart several police officers faced them. One stepped out. "Fellows, you are all under arrest."

Allister glided forward with exaggerated steps. "Officer, there must be some mistake. We are merely having a few cocktails and some snacks."

The other officers stepped out, with the lead man yelling, "Two of you stay here and entertain these guys. You others come with me and search the place."

Buster had eased himself and Shayla back down the hall. "Open that door like you did before."

Shayla grabbed the doorknob with both hands

and did an aggressive turn and shake. "Sorry, it won't budge."

An officer's voice split the air. "Hey, you! Stay right there."

Buster pushed Shayla aside and savagely twisted the doorknob.

The officer dashed toward him.

Buster grabbed Shayla as a shield. "Stay back if you don't want this slut to get hurt."

She side-stepped toward the bend of his arm that was crooked around her neck. She pulled her arm forward and forcefully shot her elbow back into the center of his belly. He doubled in pain with a big gasp. Shayla grabbed his wrist from around her neck and twisted underneath it, bending his arm as she did.

The officer reached her and cuffed the hand she held. He spun Buster around and cuffed his other hand behind his back. "Good work, miss."

"Thank you, officer, where are the other girls?"

He grinned. "They ran down the fire exit, right into the lobby full of Police Officers who had just come from a seminar on Human Trafficking. After they told us where they came from and what was going on up here, we had to toss a coin to see who got the privilege of cuffing these slime-balls. I won." He smiled. "Are you okay?"

Shayla returned the smile. "Yes, sir. I'm fine. Thank you for coming."

He leaned forward and whispered. "Abba said it was going to be an exciting day full of surprises," and he winked.

Shayla laughed. "He's always full of surprises."

The officer pushed Buster ahead, but spoke gently to Shayla. "Come this way, miss."

"May I go to the restroom first?"

"Sure thing. We'll wait near the elevator for you."

She entered the bathroom, but before she could decide what to do, a portal opened next to her and sucked her in.

Chapter 11

False Assurances

Plopping onto a hard cotton mattress, Shayla found herself on a top bunk. No one was around so she climbed down and went through a pile of clothes in a basket at the end of the room, a baggy, flowered dress, was folded neatly on top. She glanced in all directions, then wriggled her way out of the tight, knit dress and donned the flowered sack, hiding the black dress under the other clothes. A small nearby mirror reminded her of the heavy eye makeup that still marred her face. The underneath side of her dress became the closest thing to a wash cloth she could find and a little spit helped de-smudge her, just in time, as voices approached.

Giggles streamed through the doorway announcing the arrival of several young teenaged girls. The first one in, stopped, the group behind her did the same. "Who are you? Are you a new wife candidate?"

Shayla slumped her shoulders and stared at the floor. "A what? But I am new."

The girl stepped forward. "Hi, I'm Wanda. Don't you know that Jason is choosing a wife today, we're all praying that we will be *The One*, I figured your momma brought you here to be one of the Chosen Ones."

"Hi, Wanda, I'm Shayla. How can I be one of 'the chosen ones,' if he's only choosing one?"

All of them giggled, but a different girl announced. "Wow, silly—you are new, aren't you? Jason is the Anointed One and each time he chooses a wife, he gets to pick three others to be with him. We're all hoping if we aren't *The One,* we'll at least be one of the three Chosen Ones."

Shayla's back straightened. "*Each time* he chooses a wife?"

The girls began to give Shayla questioning looks and murmuring spread through the group.

Wanda asked, "Who are you? You know nothing of our ways?"

To try and ease some tension, Shayla smiled. "I have been sent by the true Sovereign to be sure that you know who the true Anointed One is."

Wanda laughed and looked at the other girls. "Of course, we know! Like I said, Jason is."

"No, I'm afraid not, Wanda. The true Anointed

One is named Jesus and his Father, the true Sovereign King, sent Him to die for your sins, to set you free?"

"To die for our sins? What sins and who killed him?"

Shayla scanned the faces of the group. "That's a little more complicated, sit down and I'll explain it to you."

An hour or so later, Shayla finished by saying, "So you see, Jason is an imposter. He's been deceiving you and others, for years."

At that instant, a man bolted through the door. "You're the liar and deceiver. Get away from my flock."

Shayla stood and faced the man. "You must be Jason and *no*, I am not the deceiver. I speak the truth. You lie to these girls to satisfy your own lust and you keep them in ignorance so they will be your willing sex slaves, but not anymore, Jason, your deception is over. They have heard the truth now it will be confirmed with miraculous signs."[xx]

Jason pulled a whip from his hip pocket.

She raised her palm to face him. "No weapon formed against me will prosper, that is my heritage."[xxi]

"We shall see, you impudent hussy." He raised his whip overhead and took a step, the fall portion of the whip dangled down his back into the floor behind him.

Shayla leaned into her outstretched palm, pushed it toward Jason, and shouted, "Neither you nor your whip will touch me or these girls. I bind it, in the name of Jesus!"

As if a wind pushed him, he staggered a step back, when he tried to regain his stance the split-tipped cracker at the end of the whip wrapped around his leg. As he yanked, the length of the whip tightened, his arm became taut and the leather seized his ankle, tearing away a bit of flesh. A stream of vile curse words poured from Jason's lips.

The girls gasped at the unexpected eruption.

"Girl, I will thrash you!" Jason shouted.

Shayla leaned into her outstretched palm even tighter. "If you come any closer, you will know the wrath of the true and living God."

He lunged toward her, but his entrapped ankle jerked the weighted handle and thong from his hand, propelling them downward, striking him on the head. His eyes fluttered and he toppled to the floor.

Shayla relaxed her arm. "Girls, you have witnessed what the Almighty God can do. You are now free from this pretender and you are forgiven for being deceived. I'll call the local authorities to help reunite you with your families." She reached for the whip and used it to bind Jason's hands and feet behind him. "Wanda, where is the office?"

Within half an hour, local officials arrived to take Jason into custody and to help the girls locate their parents.

The local Sheriff walked toward Shayla and lifted his hand. "We want to thank you for your help, miss. We've been looking for a way to break this cult, but up till now, we've been shut out by the folks that live here. It's sad to say, but many of these girls are no more than twenty miles from home."

Shayla lifted her hand in response, he clasped it with both of his.

"My pleasure, Sheriff. I'm glad that these girls now know the truth. Is there a church in town that you can refer them to, to get some counseling?"

"I'd be delighted, young lady. My son's the pastor of one and he and some others can provide what these people need."

About that time, Federal Marshal, Lydia Fleetwood came in, walked over to the pair and greeted the Sheriff. "Hi, Luke, thanks for inviting me in on this raid." She shifted her glance to Shayla and asked her name, when she replied, Fleetwood tipped her head a little to the side. "You're Shayla McKnight? That name showed up in an online report from the gulf coast of Texas."

"Yes ma'am, Marshal. I was there."

Fleetwood looked over her shoulder to her

partner in the room, then turned back to Shayla. "But honey, this is Wilmington, Idaho. How could you possibly be here?"

In her spirit, Shayla heard, "Go to the bathroom."

"Will you excuse me, I need to go to the Ladies' Room."

"Go ahead, but we need to get you to our headquarters immediately."

Shayla smiled and headed to the door in the back corner of the room. She walked in and closed it behind her. "Abba, what am I going to do? Should I have lied about my name?" With both hands behind her, she leaned against the door. A soothing reply came into her spirit.

"No need to tell a lie, Mighty One."

The air began to spin around her.

"Where to now, Ab …?"

Chapter 12

To the Desert

Unbearably hot air greeted Shayla as she dropped onto dry sand. "This is different."

A tarantula scurried away, only inches from her feet. Stifling air burned her nostrils, blistering sun beat down, her hands stung against the broiling-hot sand as she pushed herself up. Rocks, sand dunes, cactus, beige mountains and glaring sun filled every inch of space within her view. "What now, Abba? Where do I go?"

In her spirit came the words, *walk away from the sun.*

She chuckled to herself. "Thank goodness it isn't high noon or I'd be totally confused." She moved to position the sun to her back. At least the long, baggy flowered dress offered some protection, but the thirst, "Abba, what am I to do about that?"

A sparkle caught her attention, a north-facing

crevice in a rock held a small handful of water. She bent to sip from the pool, then folded some of the cloth at the bottom of her dress and sopped up the remaining moisture. She sucked on the fabric to get as much of the water as possible and used the damp spot to wipe her face.

When she raised her head, two small pairs of eyes stared at her. One tiny voice asked, "Did you drink it all? We drank some last night, but saved the rest for this morning."

Shayla's eyes widened. "Oh, my goodness, I'm sorry …"

But the second girl, slightly older, interrupted. "No look, there's some left." She pointed to the crevice in the stone. "Do you mind if we get a little drink?"

Shayla's eyes darted toward the rock, in her spirit she whispered, *Thank you, Abba*. Then turned to the children. "Please drink as much as you need."

As soon as the girls finished drinking, Shayla dipped a fresh spot on her hem into the remaining water. "Come here, let me wipe your faces."

The small, angel-like countenances smiled up at her. The moist cloth must have felt good, each girl sighed as the smooth, damp fabric wiped away the dust.

Shayla moved the younger girl back to arm's length and rested her hands on the thin shoulders. "Where did you girls come from? Do you live around here?"

The older girl pointed into the west. "There's a house out yonder, my sister and I were taken to it one night and we ain't seen our momma or daddy since. They told us it was a school, but we ain't learned nuthin yet."

Shayla's shoulders pulled back. "Who took you there?"

The smaller girl replied. "We never seen who it was. It was dark when they taked us from our house, me and Matty runned away last night. They was mean to us and didn't give us food unless we did ever-thin they said."

She turned to the older child. "So, you are Matty?"

"Yes, 'um."

Shayla bent low to be closer to the younger child. "And what's your name, sweet girl?"

"I'm Leona."

"Okay, Leona and Matty, you stick with me and let's see if we can't find a better place." When she straightened, a cloud of dust stirred in the distance. "Looks like we may have some help coming."

Matty tiptoed, then frowned. "No ma'am, that'll be Griffin, lookin' for us."

Shayla's palms went out to her sides. "Who's Griffin?"

"He's the man who owns the school. He'll be purdy mad when he gits here, cuz we ran away. We won't git no supper tonight."

With her shoulders pulled back, Shayla said, "We'll see about that. Anyway, we can't stay out here in the desert, we'll die of thirst or starvation." She raised her hand to flag the driver of the jeep.

Seconds later, the vehicle slid to a dusty stop in front of them. "Girl, did you take my kids?"

Her chin rose and so did her voice. "No, and my name is Shayla, not girl. They were lost and I was trying to help them."

"Looks more like you're the one who's lost. Matty and Leona, you've been very bad, runnin' away like that. You could have died out here."

Matty's small voice yelled, "I'd rathern die out chere than to die at your school. We heard yous talkin' on the phone. You ain't gonna harvest our innerds and sell our guts to nobuddy."

Griffin's mouth pulled up at one corner. "You girls been dreamin' again. I'm not sellin' anybody's innerds." His nervous eyes flashed at Shayla, then back to the girls. "Honestly, lady, I don't know where these girls get their notions."

Shayla smiled. "Then take us to the nearest town and we'll get this all sorted out."

The man's eyes shifted side-to-side. "Yes ma'am, sure thing. You and the girls get in the car and we'll do just that." He leaned over, opened the front door and pushed the seat forward. "Climb in."

Leona crawled in first. Shayla held Matty's hand to be sure the man didn't try to drive off with the two girls and leave her behind. Once they settled into the back seat, Griffin threw the jeep into gear, turned around and they roared back the way he'd come.

After only a few minutes, Matty looked up at Shayla. "He ain't takin' us to town, ma'am." She pointed back to a road they had past. "Town's that-a-way."

Shayla dove forward and grabbed the back of Griffin's seat. "I said to take us to town."

"We need to go home and get the girls some clean clothes first. I don't want those Ya-hoos in town thinking I'm not takin' care of the children at the school. Settle down, we'll be there any minute."

Shayla leaned back, but looked at Matty who shook her head. That pushed her to a quick, silent prayer. Abba, you know where we are and why I'm here. Please give me wisdom and direction. In Jesus' name, amen.

The vehicle wheeled into the yard of a large, drab house. Griffin yelled. "Everybody out. Girls take this lady to my office and you both get back to the dorm."

She tried to protest, but the man grabbed her firmly by the upper arm. "You are coming with me." He opened the door to an office furnished with a desk, a high back chair and two hard, ladder-back chairs.

"Now what are you doin' out here and why'd you have them girls with you?"

Shayla eased herself onto one of the chairs. "I'd lost my way and the two girls found me. I was going to take them into town to attempt to find their parents when you came roaring up."

He jabbed his index finger down on the desk. "Them kids are supposed to here at this school."

Cutting her eyes up at him, she said, "I realize this is a fine school, I can tell by your eloquent grammar and by the tasteful decor."

Griffin's hand drew back, but he caught himself. "Listen, Miss. These children here have been voluntarily placed in my care by their parents and I have sworn to tend to them. I can't have them traipsing off into the desert, now can I?"

She clinched her fists. "When the parents *voluntarily* placed their children in your care, did they know that you are an illiterate barbarian who beat them and never taught them anything but fear and hunger?"

Rage gripped him. He lashed out, but Shayla slid from the chair and ducked. She scrambled to her feet. "Don't hit me, you brute!"

The door swung open and a tall lean woman in jeans and a shirt grabbed Shayla by the arm. "We don't have time for this, Grif. We have customers on the way." She struggled, but managed to drag

Shayla from the room. Down the hall a door was open and Shayla was shoved into a room with other girls, younger than herself.

Matty stepped forward. "Well, at least you're still in one piece. I feared he'd chop you into bits. That's what he threatens to do to us if we yell or anythin."

Shayla scanned the girls. "I'm glad you and Leona are all right. Who are your friends?"

"They's other girls who's been left into the ker of Griffin and his wife Godzilla."

"What did she mean by customers are on their way? What customers?"

"They's people that when they come, some of the girls go to meet them and we never sees 'em agin."

Shayla bent close to Matty's face. "Do you know if they leave with the people?"

"No ma'am, we don't know. All I've ever heard is a man say to Griffin, 'You've got a fine stable here,' but we don't got no horses or nuthin. Just us girls."

"Matty, what did you mean when you said they weren't going to harvest your innerds or sell your guts?"

"I heared one man say his daughter needed a new heart and this was the only place he'd been able to find one. Well, I know he wasn't gonna git it from Griffin or Godzilla, cus they don't have even one heart betweents 'em. One of the girls, Tragen, was taken to him and Griffin assured him that she was a perfect match."

She touched Matty's shoulders. "How did he know she was a match?"

"I dun't know, but the man said sumthin about a spider's web."

Shayla frowned. "Spider's web? Do you think he could have meant a website?"

"I dun't know, ma'am, but sumthin about a web, later I heared Griffin on the phone with Tragen's folks. He said she'd been picked to attend some fancy private school back East, all spenses paid."

Shayla stood erect and began to pace. "This place must be a black-market organ farm." She turned to the girls. "Did they do a blood test on you?"

Another girl answered. "Yes, um. Every girl here has to be tested to be sure they's healthy."

Shayla stomped her foot. "These devils!" She turned to face the door. "Father, what am I to do? How do I stop these wicked people?"

Matty tugged at her skirt. "Are you okay ma'am or has the heat got to ya?"

About that time, they heard a car pull up out front. The engine was turned off and the door slammed. Footsteps hit the porch that sounded heavy, like a man's.

Griffin must have met him.

A voice echoed through the open door. "Mr. Griffin, you are a God-send."

Shayla couldn't bare it. She tried the door knob, but it was locked. She beat on the door and yelled, "God has nothing to do with this place! Stop what you're doing!"

The woman came to the door and shoved it open, propelling Shayla backwards to the floor. She grabbed one of the girls and hauled her through the opening, slamming and locking it behind her.

Shayla stared up from the floor, unable to fathom what she knew was about to happen.

Matty bent to help her up.

Groaning, Shayla picked herself up and faced the group. "We have got to get you all out of here, but I don't know how yet.

An engine roared and turned out of the yard.

Matty asked, "Where'd that there bird come from?"

Shayla listened intently, then faced the girls. "I can't get you all out at once, but Matty and Leona are in danger right now. I have to get them out first. I'll do my best to get you all to safety. Do you understand?"

Blank faces stared at her and nodded *yes*, just as the door swung inward.

Godzilla screamed, "Everyone on the front porch!"

The group moved as a single unit, scurrying

through the doorway and down the hall. Griffin met them on the outside the front door.

"Cassy, you and Fiona, draw some water and take it to the kitchen."

The girls dashed to the side of the porch and lowered the bucket into the well. The handle squeaked as they drew up a fresh batch of water.

"Take it to the kitchen and hurry back, the well water is going to be a little muddy for a while." He glared at Shayla.

She lowered her head between Matty and Leona and whispered, "Girls, do exactly as I tell you, no matter how crazy it sounds. Okay?"

The girls nodded.

After the water bucket had been taken to the kitchen, Griffin took the well-rope and attached a seat that looked like a swing.

"Uh-oh," said Matty.

Shayla whispered again, "Don't worry, just do exactly as I tell you."

Griffin grabbed Shayla by the elbow and spun her with her back toward him. He bound her wrists behind her with a zip tie and pulled the seat toward her. "Sit down," and pushed her toward the swing. "Girls, about four of you hold the handle till I get there."

Shayla scooted over and delicately seated herself.

Griffin pushed the seat off the porch and she

dangled over the well opening. When he reached the handle, the girls parted and he began lowering the swing bearing Shayla into the mouth of the well.

When Shayla's head began to lower below the rim, she yelled, "Matty, Leona, jump for the rope and hold on."

Griffin saw the two girls launch themselves from the porch and onto the rope. "Well looky here. We get three for one today." He sped up the mechanism until he heard a splash, then lowered them more to take into account the height of the girls holding onto the rope. "That should pretty much do it."

Suddenly the rope went slack.

Shayla, Matty and Leona heard a splash and landed on a concrete floor. Behind them, jail cells, stood open awaiting their next occupants.

Matty looked around. "Oh, boy, looks like we're gonna to be put in jail."

A man's voice drew their attention toward the office door. "What the tarnation? Who the heck are y'all?"

Shayla lifted her eyes to meet the man's face. "Could you help me up and I'll gladly tell you the whole story."

He reached for her hand, but saw that they had been bound behind her and she sat in a puddle of water. Her hair and clothes dripped into the pool.

He pulled a knife from his pocket, Matty and Leona's mouths flew open and they hopped back. "Don't worry, little gals, I'm the Sheriff and I won't hurt you." He plucked the tie from Shayla's wrist and reached again to help her up.

When she got to her feet, she rubbed her hands to restore the circulation. "Thank you, Sheriff."

"Now let's start with how you got here and how you brought a slosh of water with you." He pulled up a chair and gestured for her to sit down.

She looked at his face with searching eyes. "Sheriff, do you know the Lord?"

He pulled his shoulders back. "Well, yes I do, but what does that have to do with anything?"

"It's going to make it a lot easier to explain." She pointed to the girls. "These girls and others are being held at a so-called school outside of town."

"Yeah, I know the place. Poor people round here send their girls there to try and give 'em a better life."

"Actually, what they are doing is sending those girls to their doom. That man Griffin and his wife are using a website to match people who need organ transplants with those girls and selling them on the internet."

"What? You gotta be kidding? I've met the man, he's no rocket scientist, but he seemed like a nice-enough fellar."

Shayla continued to rub her wrists. "He's a good

actor at best. He's the one who bound my hands and he put me on a plank and lowered me into a well. I told the girls to jump onto the rope as it was going down. God saved us by *shifting us here*, I guess you could say. I don't know if he meant to drown me or just scare me, but Abba saw fit to get us out. What I need for you to do is to get a search warrant and seize his computer. I'm sure he doesn't know where we are, but you need to hurry. And if you could contact the U.S. Marshal's Office they can add this to a list of events that they and the FBI are investigating."

The Sheriff placed his hands on his waist. "And I'm supposed to do all of that on your say-so, am I?"

Shayla folded her arms. "If you don't believe me, call the U.S. Marshal's Office in Wilmington, Idaho and ask for Federal Marshal Lydia Fleetwood, but please hurry. She'll tell you that I'm telling the truth or you can lock me up."

Looking at Matty and Leona the Sheriff asked, "So is this the truth?"

Matty nodded, but Leona said, "How else do you splain us sittin in a puddle of water in your jail, Mr. Sheriff."

He grunted and turned to his office. "Do you girls want to sit on the porch and dry off a spell, while I'm on the phone?"

They walked to the door and Shayla cracked it

open. She looked both ways before opening it more.

The Sheriff observed her behavior and rang the operator. "Give me the number for the U.S. Marshal's Office in Wilmington, Idaho."

Moments later, he walked onto the porch and stood before the girls. "Deputy Fleetwood is anxious to talk to you, miss. She confirmed your story, but can't figure out how you got away from her and ended up here. She said it beat the daylights outta her." He smiled, leaned in and said, "Lord only knows."

The Sheriff ordered some food from the diner and brought the girls inside for safe keeping. "Now Miss Shayla, are you going to hang around for the execution of the search warrant I've ordered?"

She leaned toward him and smiled. "Well Sheriff, the Lord only knows."

After the food arrived and the girls had filled their bellies, Shayla asked, "May I use your restroom, Sheriff?"

"Let me at least shake your hand first, little lady. Fleetwood said that's how she lost you." He grinned and trapped her hand between his two giant paws. "It's been nice to meet ya, Shayla. I'll take good care of these girls and the others."

"Thank you, Sheriff." She entered the restroom and leaned against the sink. "Well, Father, have I missed my mother's wedding? Is she worried about me? I trust you, but when will I get back home?"

The sink began to wobble, her eyes flew open, it felt like she was being pulled backwards into the basin. The next thing she knew … .

Chapter 13

A Dark Metal Can

Shayla landed with knees bent, her feet out in front of her bottom which rested on a hard metal floor, her elbows bent and hands behind her. The container lurched to the side and she slid into someone. "Who's there?"

A man's grunt echoed around her.

She moved away, but bumped into another person. "Where am I?"

"Senorita, what are you doin' here?"

"I don't know. I mean, I'm not sure. Where are we?"

"We are being sent to work in the city, where we will have nice jobs and nice houses. When we save enuff money, we will send for our families."

"We? Who are you or how many are in here? Where did you come from?"

"We came from many countries and paid a coyote to get us across the border."

"You paid a what?"

"The men who sneaks us across in cars or trucks are knowed as coyotes."

The darkness settled in on Shayla, she prayed silently. "Father, what am I doing here? Wherever here is." The truck hit a large pothole, she bounced and collided with the man with whom she had been speaking.

"Senorita, I thought this group was all men. How did you get in here? I didn't see any chica when I climbed in."

Stammering for something that made sense, she replied. "I don't know, I got confused and I ended up here. When will we stop, do you know?"

"When we clear the checkpoint and arrive at our new jobs, we will stop."

"But how long will that take?"

The sound of brakes accompanied a shift of bodies. Footsteps outside grew louder and the rear cargo door creaked open.

A splash of light caused her to squint.

A gruff voice croaked, "Okay hombres, this is the end of the line."

Shayla nestled behind the man who had kindly answered her questions. Men crawled toward the doorway. Many voices rumbled. Her shield also slid toward the opening.

His familiar voice questioned. "Amigo, what is dis place?"

Two rows of low buildings stretched out on either side of the transport truck.

"Dis is not the city."

"This is it, amigo. Now, out!"

Begrudgingly the man scooted across the opening, his feet hit the ground in a light puff of dust.

The gruff voice echoed into the almost empty container. "What have we here? A purddy little gal in a tater sack dress. How'd you get in there, girl? You gals ain't supposed to be here till later this afternoon. Did they send you ahead to cook us some dinner?" He laughed. "Git over here."

Shayla scrambled to the doorway.

The man leaned into her face, but pointed toward one of the buildings. "The kitchen is thatta way." His breath reeked of tobacco and onions. "Now skedaddle." He grabbed her arm and yanked her from the trailer.

She trembled before him.

Again, he yelled, "Git, vamos!"

Darting toward the building, she glanced over her shoulder at the young tan-faced man who stood bewildered, staring back at her. A tractor, pulling an open wagon pulled into the compound.

The gruff voice again barked out orders. "Okay, amigos, it's time to go to work." He pointed at the waiting farm equipment and smacked his hands together. "Arriba, arriba! Andale, andale!"

Brown-faced men scurried toward the waiting wagon, except for the young man.

"What's the matter, chico? Are you deaf?"

"Senor, we were promised good jobs in the city."

Stained teeth grinned at him. "That comes later, seen-yor. Now move it."

Shayla watched as the vicious man snatched the arm of the young man and propelled him toward the waiting tractor.

He fell to the ground.

A powerful kick greeted his ribs. "Now, git up and move!"

Helpless, the young man crawled to his knees and stood, holding his side. His eyes met Shayla's.

She motioned for him to go to the tractor.

He turned and stumbled to the rear where he was lifted aboard by several strong hands.

"Abba, father, what am I to do? Give me wisdom."

A soothing familiar voice entered her ear. "Prepare some food, the men will need nourishment."

Through the door, she found the kitchen and located the pantry. Most of the cans' labels were in Spanish, but drab pictures revealed the contents.

"I don't know how to cook these, Abba." But a

calmness filled her spirit. She kicked off her shoes and located a large sack of beans, washed them, then filled a kettle with water. The gas stove whooshed into flame below the pot.

Within minutes, the water began to boil, she lowered the fire and scoured the kitchen for more food. She lined the counter with tortillas in plastic bags, an orangey sauce, onions and what looked like green tomatoes with papery skins. She plopped a spoonful of lard into a skillet, chopped some onions, a few of the green things and fried them together. Bowls, glasses and spoons were located. It felt like hours had passed.

She stirred the beans and tasted them. "Soft, but flavorless. Salt, now where is the salt?" Her hands lifted lids and white substances were tasted. "Umm, sugar. A handful of this will help, but where is the salt."

A mild young voice said, "Over there in the tin can."

Shayla slapped her hand on her chest and whirled around to see a boy, less than half her age, standing behind her. "You scared me! Who are you?"

"Hi, I'm Roscoe. Most of the girls round here don't speak English. Where'd you come from?"

"That's a long story, Roscoe. What are you doing here?"

"My uncle owns this farm."

"Oh, so is your mother or father around?"

Roscoe shoved his hands in his pockets. "No, they died in a car crash a few years back, so I came here to live with Uncle Bill and Aunt Peggy."

"I'm sorry to hear that, Roscoe, so is your aunt nearby?"

Roscoe's face tipped toward the floor. "Nah, she died last year. She was never very strong and they said her heart just gave out on 'er."

"Oh, my goodness, I'm so sorry. You've had a lot of loss in your life for such a young boy."

"Aunt Peggy couldn't have kids of her own and she told me that I was the only thing in the world that kept her goin." He looked up and smiled. "She used to read to me and we would sit and talk for hours. She said I was a gift from heaven and that my hair was the same color as hers when she was a girl. Said it reminded her of a soft sunset."

"That was sweet of her and I'm sure it's true, but who takes care of you now?"

Roscoe drew an invisible circle on the floor with the toe of his boot. "Don't need nobody else, it's just me and Uncle Bill now."

"But Roscoe, do you know what your uncle does here on the farm?"

He pulled his hands from his pockets and tipped his chin up. "Sure, I do, stupid. He's giving these poor people a better life. They get food, a place to sleep and they don't have to worry about nuthin."

Shayla tried to be gentle, she placed one hand on his shoulder. "You know, Roscoe, that's not exactly true."

A stern tone entered his voice. "Sure it is and you'd better finish cookin.' The tractor'll be bringing the men back from the field any minute now."

The tone of his voice snapped her to attention. She grabbed a handful of sugar and tossed it into the pot and dumped in a handful of salt. "I hope that's enough."

"You'd better throw in some of these chili peppers and dump in that skillet of onions and tomatillos."

Shayla followed his orders and stirred the pot. With a clean spoon she tasted the brew. "Hmmm, this is not bad."

Moments later, the door at the end of the room swung open. Dusty, sweaty men lumbered into the dining hall.

Roscoe poured water into a large keg with a spigot. He began filling glasses to the brim. Men rushed forward and gulped the water, refilling their glasses.

A familiar gruff voice barked, "Enough, Hombres! Get yore food and make it snappy."

With grimy hands, each man picked up a bowl, spoon and tortilla, they shuffled through the line like zombies, each receiving a large ladle-full of beans. A few paused to plop some orange sauce on top before sliding onto the hard, rough benches.

Shayla's eyes searched the tired faces. "Is that all they're going to get?"

"Look girly, that's more than they'd git back home. They'll be grateful."

The silent band of men, leaned over their bowls and dipped into the beans. One-by-one they looked up with wide eyes and stared at her.

"What's wrong?" she whispered.

"Nothing, senorita," replied a friendly voice. "We aren't use to such delicioso food."

Shayla stared at him. "So, it's good? I'm glad, because I'm not much of a cook."

White teeth beamed from his dusty face. "Only mi abuela, mi grandmutter, you would say, could do better. This is excelente!"

"Then Abba did the cooking!" she chuckled.

"Abba, senorita, you know Abba?"

"Si, I mean, yes. He's why I'm here."

The young man tilted his head. "I dun't understand. You are here because of Abba?"

"Yes, I'm here to help you."

"How senorita, how can you help us?"

She tucked her chin. "Well, I don't know yet, but he'll show me, I'm sure of it."

A thunderous voice shouted, "Okay, enough! Git back to the wagon."

Men scurried to down the last of their beans and water.

The young man lifted the bowl to his mouth and scooped in the remaining beans. "Thank you, senorita. For the first time in days, I feel nutrir and contento."

Shayla squinched her face. "Nutrir?"

"Hmm, you might say, nourish'd and satisfied. Thank you, bonita lady. My name is Mateo."

Shayla smiled. "I'm Shayla and you're welcome." She leaned toward him. "And I'll be working on a plan to get you out of here."

The voice boomed again, "Okay, senor Romeo, get to the wagon."

The smile melted from Mateo's face, he turned and marched toward the door. The line of men trudged from the dining hall.

Roscoe appeared at Shayla's side. "Not bad for a gringo! That was good grub."

Shayla's nose wrinkled. "Gringo?"

"Yeah, you know, a Yank, an American, someone who's not Hispanic."

"Oh, gotcha. Now Roscoe, I need your help."

He threw his hands up in front of him. "Nope, I'm not doing dishes! There'll be a load of gals coming in soon that can help you with that."

Shayla giggled. "Not that kind of help, silly. Look at me."

The boy scanned her head to toe.

"Can't you tell that I don't belong here?" She slowed her speech and bent her shoulders to his eye level. "Look Roscoe. Someone put me in that last truck and I need to get home. I'm not one of these people who needs your uncle's kind of help. Can't you see that?"

He stared at the floor. "What cha want me to do?"

"My name is Shayla, you can call me Shay. I need to use a phone. Can you help me?"

He waggled his head. "I don't know, Shay. Uncle Bill would wallop me good if I let you in the house."

"Then could you make a call for me? It'll be a Texas number. It's my … my cousin Beau. He'll come and get me. You can sneak him in and your uncle will never know, okay? Here's his number." Shayla pulled a plain blank piece of paper and a pencil from a drawer. On it she wrote Beau, 361-555-7777 and shoved it at Roscoe.

"You gonna get the fire beat outta me."

"No, Beau will make everything alright for you. I promise! He's great like that. Just call him, that's his private number, but he'll say some kind of funny prank statement when he answers it. He may say, county morgue or state police or Joe's Bar. Just ignore what he says and tell him his cousin Shayla needs him, then tell him where he can find me, but not to tell your uncle who he is when he gets here.

Can you do that? I'm sure there will be a big reward for you helping him to find his cousin."

Roscoe's eyes shot open wide. "A reward? How much?"

Shayla placed her hands on his shoulders and smiled. "Oh, you can never tell, but I assure you, your life will never be the same. Now scoot and don't let your uncle catch you. That will increase your reward."

Roscoe smiled, walked to the door and turned to look at Shayla. "You promise?"

"I promise your life will never be the same! Cross my heart."

He opened the door a crack, peeked out and bolted toward the main house.

Shayla prayed. "Abba, help him follow through and not get caught." Through the dusty window, Shayla saw Bill heading for the house. She pushed the door open and ran toward the road.

Bill yelled, "Git back here you idjit. There ain't nuthin' out there but cactus."

Shayla quickened her pace, Bill had no option but to jump in the jeep and follow her. By the time he got it cranked, she had quite a lead on him, but the vehicle roared down the road after her. When he reached her, she was out of breath and slowed her pace to a walk.

"What in the Sam-hill do you think you're doin?"

Shayla propped her hands at her waist and gulped for air. "Just looking for the bathroom, that's all."

"Get in you idjit. I'll show you to the outhouse." The jeep roared into the compound, Bill cut the engine, he walked to her side and grabbed her arm, pulling her to the ground.

Behind the rear of the jeep, Shayla saw Roscoe come out of the house and sit down on the steps. She watched as he gave a small thumbs up gesture. She tipped her thumb up in return as Bill jerked her to a standing position.

"Don't make me beat you, girl. Now git in there and wash them dishes. A truck load of gals will be here any minute and they'll need some grub."

Shayla rubbed her arm where Bill's thumbprint throbbed under the skin, but she made her way to the kitchen. "Thank you, Abba and make my words to Roscoe true in the most beautiful way. In Jesus' name, amen." She sailed into washing the dishes with a song in her heart, knowing that Abba was in control.

After a few minutes and a stack of clean dishes, a truck rolled into the courtyard and came to an abrupt stop.

Bill met the driver. "Any problems?"

"None that I couldn't take care of, Bill."

The driver flung open the double back doors and

turned to his cargo. "Okay, girls, here's your passport to a better life. Go to the kitchen and get some food."

Girls of all sizes, hopped down from the truck. They squinted and glanced around, but the man pointed.

"Food, la comida, vamos!"

A line of frightened faces staggered toward the dining hall.

Shayla hurried to fill glasses. When the door opened, Shayla lifted a glass and shouted, "Agua."

Girls ran and desperately stumbled toward the liquid. Gulps and sighs echoed in the sparsely furnished room.

Shayla stepped behind the counter and began to fill bowls. "Father, please provide enough food for all of these girls."

Bowl after bowl was filled and Shayla peeked into the pot. She tilted her face toward the ceiling and whispered, "Thank you, Father."

The sound of a helicopter whirred overhead until it landed in the field behind the wooden building.

A shout, through a megaphone, filled the air. "Shayla, Miss McKnight! Are you here?"

Roscoe slid in behind her. "Your cousin is a hoot. You were right, when he answered his phone, he said, U.S. Marshal Beau Johnson. Now he shows up in a helicopter, shouting for his cousin, calling you Miss McKnight. He's funny and he must be some kinda rich."

The door at the end of the room burst open. His pearly white smile greeted her, "Well, cousin, I see you've gotten yourself into another scrape."

"Beau, these girls just arrived and there are men in a field somewhere. Be sure to take care of them."

"Already done, cousin. Now introduce me to the fine young man who called me."

Shayla placed her hand on Roscoe's back and faced him. "This is my hero, Roscoe. He lives with his Uncle Bill, because his parents were killed in an accident, but he could see that I didn't belong here. He risked a great deal to help me."

"Actually, Miss McKnight, we checked into who was calling and found his name on the Missing Persons' Registry. Seems his mother has been looking for him for about five years."

Roscoe's eyes widened. "Huh? Uncle Bill said my parents were dead."

Beau leaned his tall frame to the boy's face and placed his hand on his shoulder. "No son, your mom never gave up looking for you. You were taken from a grocery cart when you were two. The small store had no cameras, so there were no leads until now. Not only did you rescue Shayla, but," he stood and swept his hand across the room, "you've rescued all of these girls and the men in the field. You are quite a hero, young man."

The sound of an approaching siren pulled their attention to the center of the courtyard. A screech of tires, a cloud of dust, then a door opened and a woman's voice erupted. "Roscoe, Roscoe! Are you here?"

The door flew open again, a woman with wild eyes and tousled hair burst through. Her eyes searched the room and landed on the young man next to Shayla. She worked her way through the room and stood before him. "Yes, it's your eyes, your hair, your face, but older." She cupped her hands around his cheeks. "You may not recognize me, but I'm your mom."

Tears filled Roscoe's eyes. "I know your voice. It's different, but the same."

"I've been crying because I was so excited that you'd been found, but I assure you, I know you. You're my son."

Beau rested his hand on the small shoulder again. "Son, I assure you, this woman has looked for you for years and we will do a DNA test just to be certain."

Roscoe shuffled forward and threw his arms around the woman's waist. He moaned, "Momma, Momma, I've missed you."

She sobbed into his hair.

Shayla wiped her eyes and looked into Beau's face. "I had no idea what Abba meant when he told me to tell Roscoe that his life would never be the same." She burst into tears and leaned into Beau's chest, her head rested just under his chin.

He placed his hands on her back in a comforting, gentlemanly manner until she was able to gather herself.

She pushed away, wiped her face and cleared her voice. "Beau, thank you for coming to my rescue—again."

"It is my sincere pleasure, Miss McKnight, but I would be happier if you didn't need rescuing." He stared into her eyes and smiled. "Do you think you could manage that?"

She smiled and looked down. "I will check with my travel agent."

Law Enforcement officers entered the hall and spoke to the girls in Spanish. Shayla and Beau watched from the kitchen window, as they were ushered to vans waiting in the courtyard. Roscoe and his mother were placed in a squad car and a uniformed officer started the engine. Bill and his men were cuffed and led to a different vehicle.

Beau stretched his arm toward the door. "We'd better get you home, Miss McKnight."

She stepped to the kettle on the stove. "Before we go, I want to show you something." She lifted the lid. "Look in there."

Beau leaned forward. "Smells good. Seems a shame to leave a full pot of beans."

Shayla giggled.

Beau squinted. "What am I miss here?"

She grinned and said, "I cooked those beans and fed all of the men in the field, then when the girls came in, they were all served a bowl of beans. Look! The pot is still full! I love it! Abba is so wonderful."

Beau took a spoon and dipped himself a mouthful. "Hmmm, Miss McKnight, you are quite a good cook."

She scooped out another small taste before replacing the lid. "Hmmm!" then tossed her head back, gave a hearty laugh and turned her eyes toward Beau. "I've never cooked a dried bean before in my life, but apparently onions and those green-tomato-things that Abba created make them taste really good. Every one enjoyed them."

Beau laughed and turned to scoop another spoonful. When he lifted the lid, there was only a small amount left at the bottom. "Shay-la, look!"

When she stared into the pot, her shocked eyes cut toward Beau and they both laughed.

Beau stretched his hand toward the door. "Perhaps Abba is telling us it's time to go." They walked the length of the room and Beau held the door open, but Shayla turned.

"I've got to get my shoes. Beau, you go on outside, I'll meet you."

"Okay, Miss McKnight, I'll wait for you right— out—here." The door closed behind him.

Shayla rushed to the kitchen, but when she stepped into her shoes, dry air spun around her, the floor became spongy and she slipped through.

Chapter 14

A Damp Musty Tunnel

Shayla landed in a storage area that reeked of sewage. Stacks of boxes, some filled with fabric, some with canned items, surrounded her. Various types of food, piled on trays in a rack, stood near the door.

That must be the way out of here, Shayla tiptoed to the exit and rested her head against the splintery wood. No sound came from outside the room, she turned the knob, when she peered out, a dingy kitchen lay before her. Pots and pans hung on hooks draped from the low ceiling. "Oh, no, looks like I'm cooking again." The smell of stale water drifted from the sink. Her stomach reacted to the stench and she pinched her nose closed.

A young girl's voice startled her. "You'll get used to it in time."

Shayla wheeled around. "Oh, you caught me

off-guard, I didn't hear you come in."

The girl chuckled, "Sorry, it's my turn to cook and I guess you're the clean-up girl? I haven't seen you before."

"Yeah, I'm new. I just got dropped off, you might say. I'm Shayla, but most people call me Shay."

"Hi, I'm Hobbles."

Shayla tipped her head to the side. "Hobbles, what kind of name is that?"

The girl leaned forward and took a step. Her awkward stride was exactly that, a hobble.

"Oh, I'm so sorry! I didn't know…"

"It's okay, stop your blabberin.' At least I don't have to see the Johns anymore. The guy who did this to me, did me a favor."

Shayla gasped. "Someone else told me something similar."

The young girl approached the stove. "Yeah, now all I have to do is cook or clean. I'm okay with that."

"Why didn't they throw you out? That's what the other girl told me they did to injured girls."

Hobbles laughed. "I guess they like my cookin' or the mistress has a soft spot fur me. See she found me in the gutter in some town up north, it was winter and I was nearly froze to death."

"Where's your family?" asked Shayla.

"My mom died when I was about two and my

dad finally drank himself to death when I was about ten. I was on my own, stealin' and thieven food, sleepin' in doorways to stay warm."

Shayla lifted her shoulders and spread her palms in front of her. "Why didn't someone in the town take you in or at least take you to a shelter?"

Hobbles put her hand out in front of her. "Stop right there, a shelter, no thanks, with all of their rules and religion. I didn't need that."

"But Hobbles …"

"Shut your trap, I'm in charge in here, this is *my* kitchen. We've gotta get a move-on or there won't be no supper tonight. Get over there to the pantry and bring me some stuff."

Shayla walked back to the room she had fled only moments before and opened the door. "What do you need?"

***

There wasn't much chit-chat during the meal, but after dinner and cleaning up, Shayla asked Hobbles to show her where she was supposed to go.

Hobbles walked down a low-ceilinged hallway, wetness clung to the walls and slid in dribbles down the curved metal.

Shayla looked around. "What is this, a big pipe?"

"Yep, it used to be an underground military base, but it flooded and they up and left. Weren't that nice of 'em?" Hobbles turned and smiled at Shayla.

She touched the wall. "Yeah, very nice. I wish they could have taken some of the moisture with them. This can't be good for our health."

"Health!" Hobbles tossed her head back and laughed. "You be funny, girl. This is survival, not health. We do what the man says and we get to eat and we get to sleep—sometimes."

A door swung into a long dorm room. In the dim light, Shayla saw a dozen or more pairs of eyes turn toward her.

Hobbles bellowed, "This here's a new girl, names Shay. Treat her right and show her the ropes. Right now, you'd better git ready, the top lady will be here any minute." She turned to Shayla. "You can have the bunk over mine, but go pee first, so you don't step on me during the night."

"Where's the restroom?"

"Bahaha, girl you so funny! The can's over there." Hobbles pointed to the corner. "Put the lid on it when you're done or we'll pass out from the fumes."

The door flew open again and a woman shouted, "The van's here. Get yourselves out there."

Girls scurried past as Shayla watched them.

The woman turned her attention to Shayla. "Hey newbie, why are you standing there? Come on."

"But I just got here and I cleaned the kitchen."

"Don't matter, now get out to the van." The woman turned. "See you in the morning, Hobbles."

Hobbles lifted her hand to her forehead and chopped out a salute.

Shayla walked through the door behind the other girls and it closed behind her.

***

On the van, Shayla passed row after row of young girls and chose a seat next to a small girl with red hair. "Hi, I'm Shay."

"I'm Delilah, but you can call me Dee."

"How old are you Dee?"

"They tell me to say I'm eighteen, but I'm really only eleven."

"Eleven?" Shayla whispered. She leaned back in the seat and prayed under her breath. "Abba, what am I going to do? This little girl is so young. None of these girls are older than I am. This is abominable! Give me wisdom. Help me. In the name of Jesus, amen."

Dee stared at her. "Who you talkin' to and where'd that bird come from?"

Peace flooded Shayla. As they came to the edge of a town, she stood and wobbled her way toward the driver as the van zipped ahead.

The head woman sat on the first seat on the other side of the aisle. When Shayla appeared next to the driver, the woman shouted, "What do you think you are doing? Go sit down."

Shayla glanced over her shoulder. "I'm going to ask him to stop."

The driver yelled, "Sit down, slut."

"I will not, in the name of the Lord, you stop this van."

The woman stood and reached for her shoulder, but instantly Shayla's arm flew up and her elbow shot back pounding the madam in the chin, she dropped into her seat like a sack of rocks. Shayla grabbed the steering wheel and yanked hard toward the edge of the road. The driver hit his brakes, but the van hit a tree, propelling the driver into the windshield, yet Shayla stood unmoved. She turned toward the wide-eyed girls. "Open the back exit and jump out. Run into town. Now!"

Delilah ran, reached for the handle and pushed the door open.

Girls scurried through and ran as they were told.

As Shayla reached the door, the woman regained consciousness and hurtled toward her. "Come here, you piece of trash."

Wheeling on her heels, Shayla shouted into the woman's face. "You will not touch me and you will not pursue those girls, in the name of Jesus."

The woman's eyes flew open wide, she staggered back and fell into her seat.

Shayla ran to the back and leapt from the bus, right into the arms of a policeman. Startled, she quickly gathered her composure. "Officer, these two people," she pointed to the front of the van, "have held all those girls captive and trafficked them." She pointed to the fleeing pack of youngsters.

The officer lowered her to the ground and touched the button of the radio at his collar. "Dispatch, we have a situation out here on East Main Street. I need backup and an ambulance."

Shayla stuck out her hand. "Hi, I'm Shayla McKnight."

Moments later other vehicles arrived and Shayla called the girls to come to her.

Delilah leaned toward her and tapped her shoulder.

"Yes, Dee, what is it?"

"That one over there has paid to sleep with the girls before." She pointed to a heavy man standing near his car.

Shayla leaned toward the officer who was first on the scene and who caught her as she jumped from the van. "Abba says you are a good policeman. I want you to handle this. Delilah here," she turned toward the young redhead, "she says that man over there has paid to use some of these girls."

He turned toward her. "But miss," he paused and stared at the ground, "that's the Chief."

The Chief's eyes bore down on the junior officer.

She looked at his name tag. "Davis, I want you to call the Marshal's office and ask for Beau Johnson. Report that man to him," she leaned her head toward the chief. "but keep it under your hat until Beau gets here. In the meantime, I want you to gain access to the van's GPS. Find out where it came from. All I know is that it's an abandoned Underground Military Base."

Davis nodded. "Don't worry Miss Shayla, I know where the abandoned base is located."

"There's a young girl back there that they call Hobbles because some John crippled her. She's going to need help. She has no parents."

Dee poked her again. "That's the man who crippled Hobbles." She pointed to the chief again.

"Davis, get me some help to protect Delilah and these other girls. I don't want the Chief anywhere near them. Call every female police officer and every female firefighter in the county. Get them here to help us, now."

Davis reached for his radio again. "Dispatch, get me all of the female officers and women firefighters in the county."

Dispatch came back. "Say again?"

"You heard me, Samantha and put Ted on dispatch. I need you out here NOW."

"Yes, sir. On my way."

Two minutes later, Davis introduced Samantha to Shayla. "Samantha, I want you to help get all of these girls safely back to the station."

After Ambulance workers checked out the Madame, the driver and all of the girls, they were placed in squad cars.

Shayla turned to the young officer. "Davis, I don't want a single girl out of my sight. Tell the officers to behave themselves and get this group straight to the jail, then all of the girls will be put in a conference room with me. And remember, No One, touches them."

"Yes ma'am, Miss Shayla."

At the station, every girl was accounted for and Shayla guarded them like a hen protecting her brood of chicks.

Female officers and firefighters trickled in. They received a briefing from Davis and entered the room with Shayla and the girls.

One stepped forward. "Don't worry, miss, no one will get past us. I can promise you that."

The Chief stared in through the conference room window.

Shayla glared back at him, stepped to the back of the room and called for the girls' attention. "Girls, I want you to look at me." They all turned to face her. "There will be men who try to intimidate you, but these ladies are here to protect you." Her hand swept across the sea of women standing to the side. "When these ladies take your statements, tell them the truth. Tell them everything and point your finger at any man who has touched you in an indecent way or who touched you for money. Do you understand? Do you trust me?"

Heads bobbed all around the room.

She turned to Samantha. "I'm trusting you to handle this, okay?"

Samantha placed her hand on Shayla's arm. "You can trust me. I was rescued from traffickers by Davis a few years ago."

Shayla nodded. "Abba has this all in-hand, doesn't he? Now I need to go get Hobbles, I don't think she will trust anyone else."

Davis drove Shayla to the entrance of the underground base and they walked inside. Shayla led the way to the dorm room. She tiptoed to Hobbles bedside and touched her pillow.

Hobbles head flew up. "Oh, you scared me."

"I have a surprise for you?"

"What are you up to, new girl?"

"I know who crippled you, we are taking steps to arrest him and I would like for you to come with me."

"Where to and where are the other girls?"

"They're free and they're safe. I have a crew taking care of them. Will you come with me? I won't take you to a shelter, I promise, just Davis,"

Shayla used her thumb to point behind her, "a nice lady named Samantha, me and a wonderful man named Abba that I want you to meet."

When they returned to the station, Beau stood in the doorway. He smiled. "We meet again."

Shayla straightened and her mouth dropped open. "How did you get here so fast?"

"I choppered-over with a group of female officers that heard about this situation. I should've known you'd be at the center of it."

"This case is a hard one, Beau. The Chief is one of the men who's abused these girls."

"So, I've heard. We already have him in custody."

Shayla pulled Hobbles in front of her. "This girl was crippled by him too."

Beau leaned his lanky frame toward her and shoved his hand out. "Hey, Hobbles."

She gripped his massive paw and smiled. "Beau, what's your real name?"

He pulled a face. "Gees you ask hard questions. I'll tell you mine if you tell me yours." And he grinned.

"I used to be called Holly Cleveland, cause that's where they found me, but my last name was Mason."

"Hello, then Holly Mason, I'm Beauregard Orville Johnson."

Hobbles scrunched her face. "Now I know why you go by Beau."

He tossed his head back and laughed.

Hobbles and Shayla laughed too.

Beau turned to Shayla. "What's next for you Miss McKnight?"

"After I get Hobbles settled, I still need to find my friend, Ressa."

"Ah, I can help with that. We had officers in Arkansas go to the address your friend Sharrin told us about and the kid was sitting on the front steps."

"What a relief, I was concerned about her."

"She's a tough one, the officers had to chase her several blocks before they could talk to her. She said she wasn't going anywhere without you. We told her we'd locate you and reunite the two of you."

Shayla laughed. "You should have seen her before she met Abba, she was a piece of work even then, but now … I'm proud of the girl."

"Can I offer you a ride in the chopper? We can take you to Morgan City."

Shayla smiled. "That would be different, let me check with my travel agent." She turned to the side. "Abba, what's next for me?"

Beau studied her face. "What did he say?"

"He told me to go to the bathroom because it was going to be a long trip." She smiled and walked down the corridor to the Ladies Room. "Okay,

Abba, what now?" She entered the Ladies Room and turned toward the window. "It looks like there's an ocean out there."

Chapter 15

Rough Seas

Waves lapped the side of the building, the air around Shayla spun, suddenly wood creaked beneath her feet—she felt seasick. A ship's rail appeared on one side and a cabin with a porthole on the other.

A lavish stateroom with a king-sized bed, beckoned her tired body, until a slim, ebony-skinned girl with straight, jet black hair backed through the doorway. A man with sparkling white teeth trailed in behind her, edging her closer to the bed.

A knock at the porthole glass distracted him, his attention now on the curly-haired girl in the window.

"Hey, sweetheart, do you want to join us?" His smile flashed toward Shayla.

Muffled words seeped through the closed

window. "Leave her alone!"

Storm clouds, replaced his smile. "Who do you think you are, you little tramp?"

Fierce words flew back. "I'm an agent of the Lord, now leave her alone. Back away from her and out of the cabin."

White teeth turned to white fangs of anger. "Who's going to make me sweetheart, you?"

Shayla sped toward the doorway and pounced in on him. "I said, leave her alone."

He grabbed her wrist, knelt and flung her over his shoulder. *Thud,* she landed on the bed.

But undeterred, she rolled over, scrambled to her knees, then stepped from the bed and positioned herself between the trembling girl and the six-foot tall man.

He leaned back and placed his fists at his belt. "What do you think you are going to do frizzy-top? You've seen how I can toss you like a ragdoll. Do you think either of you are going to get out of here now without giving me a piece of you?"

"I'll die first," shouted Shayla.

Glaring at her, the man whispered, "Are you going to sacrifice your little friend too?"

The terrified girl whispered, "No please, don't kill us. I will do what you say."

Shayla's arm stretched out to the side, as if to hold her back. "You will do no such thing. This man is now under the hand of the Lord."

A demonic grin filled the lower part of his face, eyes like blazing coals stared at them. "I serve only one lord and he is the lord of darkness."

Righteous fire rose inside Shayla's belly. "I plead the blood of Jesus over myself and this girl. You cannot cross the bloodline."

He stepped forward, then backed away, again he tried to reach them. He looked at the floor and screamed. "It's blood." He backed away and fled through the threshold of the room.

A long blow of breath escaped Shayla's lips. She turned to the girl. "What's your name?"

Wide eyes stared back at her. "Carra."

"Carra, are there other girls here?"

She shook her head vigorously. "There are many. We are held below deck unless summoned."

The sound of feet pounding the deck approached.

"We need to get out of here. Do you know the way to the wheelhouse, Carra?"

Again, she nodded.

"Take my hand and show me to where the radio is."

They slipped from the cabin and headed along the bulkhead to the bow. Shayla slid the door open and crept in, Carra knelt just inside the doorway. Shayla saw a man's pipe on the window sill and eased her hand up. She gripped the bowl of the pipe in her palm, then sneaking toward the man at the helm, she eased up behind him and stuck the stem of the pipe into the man's back.

"You will pick up the radio and call the Coast Guard." She placed her free hand on the man's shoulder. "No sudden moves, do you hear me?"

The man nodded, and reached for the radio. "This is the Espie One, calling the Coast Guard, come in Coast Guard."

Static crackled. "This is the Coast Guard, go ahead Espie One."

Shayla nudged the pipe at the man's back. "Tell them our coordinates and to alert the U.S. Marshal Service that there are people being trafficked onboard this boat."

The man complied.

"We read you, Espie One. We are on our way. Cut your engines and drop anchor."

The Helmsman, replaced the mic on the radio base. He reached for the controls and cut the engine. "You know this will bring the Captain running, don't you? Look, I don't agree with what these people are doing. I'm sorry I haven't had the guts to do something about it, but these guys will feed you to the fish if they catch you."

Shayla waved for Carra to come to her. "Where can we hide?"

The man slid open a shallow console panel behind him. "Do you think both of you will fit in there?"

Shayla motioned for Carra to get in. She fit, but there wasn't quite enough room for her too. She closed the door seconds before the Captain and four other men dashed onto the bridge.

"Why did you cut the engine, you idiot? We have cargo to deliver!"

Shayla rose onto her tiptoes behind the man and peered over his shoulder. "Because I told him too. If you value this man's life, you will back away."

The captain yelled to the four crewmen. "Get her. She'll add to the value of our load."

Four scowling men dove at her as lights flashed from the outside. A loud speaker blasted. "This is the United States Coast Guard, prepare to be boarded."

The four men slunk away and out the opposite door.

Armed coastguardsmen boarded the ship, their captain made her way to the bridge. "I'm Captain Doreen Chandler of the United States Coast Guard. Who's in charge here?"

The ship's captain tried to speak, but Shayla cut him off. "Not him, at least not any more. He has people down in the hold, he was taking them to be sold. She pushed her accomplice forward and loosed her grip on his shoulder. This man helped us."

Chandler looked at her. "Us?"

Shayla slid the compartment door open and a

beautiful young face emerged.

"This is Carra. She'll show you where the others are being held."

Chandler folded her arms. "And you are?"

"I'm Shayla."

"Would that be Shayla McKnight? A United States Marshal is interested in talking to you."

Shayla folded her arms. "And would that be Beau?" Then she laughed.

"I don't know what you're playing at young lady, but when a Marshal asks me to hold you for him, I plan to do just that."

***

Captain Chandler took Shayla by the elbow and guided her to the stern of the boat. A helicopter whirred overhead, in the spotlight, a familiar figure lowered himself to the deck and removed his harness.

The man stepped forward. "Captain, I'm Deputy Beau Johnson of the U.S. Marshal Service. I hope that all of the hostages have been released."

"They have Marshal and you'll be free to interview them whenever you'd like. We're taking them to the mess deck of the cruiser. It's small, but much better that the filth they were being held in. And here's the suspect you requested we hold for you." She shoved Shayla toward Beau.

He grinned and one eyebrow rose. "Yes, this suspect is slippery."

Shayla pulled her elbow away from Chandler and folded her arms. "Beau, you know very well I'm not a suspect."

Beau laughed. "But if I wanted to talk to you, I had to have you held. Now come over here with me." He remained poised, his open palm pointing to the fantail.

She swung her arms as she stepped near the rail, folded her arms across her mid-section and leaned back. "So, talk."

Beau straightened. "Miss McKnight, I cannot have a young woman running around, putting herself in danger, no matter how admirable her intentions are."

Shayla bristled. "So, how did I run here, Beau? Huh? In the middle of the ocean. By the way, which ocean is it?"

"What? You don't know where you are."

She sheepishly admitted, "No, I don't."

"How on earth did you get here, if you don't even know where here is?"

Shayla leaned away from the rail. "It's hard to explain. Can I go to the bathroom?"

"No ma'am, that's how I lost you last time. I thought you wanted to get back to Ressa."

"I do, but I need to check with … with my handler."

Beau folded his arms across his chest and lifted his shoulders. "Your *handler!* Who are you, Miss

McKnight?"

"I'm on a special assignment, that's all I can tell you."

"Let me get this straight," he ducked his chin and stared into her eyes, "So, Abba is sending you to all of these places?"

Her face jerked up to meet his eyes. "So, you think Abba is sending me to these places?"

"I certainly do, but I'm not sure I approve of placing such a young woman in danger like this."

Standing tall, she tipped her head to the side. "So, you are wiser than Abba?"

He laughed. "You *can* be difficult, can't you?"

Softening her tone, she said, "Sorry, Deputy, I didn't ask for this. I was supposed to be attending my mother's wedding to a wonderful man. I dashed into the bathroom to check my hair and makeup, then I got whisked away."

"Someone grabbed you from the bathroom?"

"Not exactly."

"Look Shayla, I need to know how these criminals are kidnapping people. Tell me what you know."

Her eyes rested on him. "This is hard to explain. Do you believe in time travel or parallel dimensions?"

Beau leaned back and ran both hands through his hair. "What? Time travel? Parallel dimensions? I don't know. Why?"

"My brothers and I have experienced being taken from one place to another through portals or vortexes."

"Don't you think it's more likely that you went into some kind of altered state of consciousness and you thought you were someplace else?"

Shayla plopped her fists at her waist. "Do I look like I'm in an altered state of consciousness to you?"

Beau hung his head. "I'm sorry, no, you look very conscious and very present at this moment, but Miss McKnight, this is a lot to take in."

She turned to the side. "Abba, what do I do now?" She listened for a minute, then turned to Beau. "Come with me." He followed her to a doorway that was closed and she reached for the metal lever to open it. "Beau, this is going to take some faith, but I want you to take my hand and don't let go until we land."

"Land? What are you going to do, jump?"

"Trust me, the way I've trusted you to take care of these girls."

He reached out and took her hand. She stepped through the low hatch and started to disappear. He yelled, "Sha," and was sucked through behind her. A short spin, and they landed on the dining deck of the Coast Guard Cruiser." Beau looked around, but instantly knew where they were. He shook his head. "Okay, I believe you."

Shayla laughed. "You can turn loose of my hand now, I'm starting to lose the feeling in my fingers."

He looked down at her frail hand in his, his face reacted to her white knuckles and he jerked away. "I'm so sorry."

A playful laugh filled the air. "Not a problem. At least we landed standing upright. Sometimes the landings can be hard."

His eyes stretched wide. "You do this all the time?"

"No, until I was whisked away from Mom's wedding, I hadn't cloud skimmed in five years."

Beau's eyebrows reached for his hairline. "Five years, you know that exactly how?"

"It's difficult to forget your first time as a Skimmer, in fact I think you'll remember this for a good, long time."

Beau rested his open hands on his hips and looked at the floor. "Indeed, Miss McKnight, indeed I will."

"I need to go to the restroom and," she looked down at herself, "I wish I had some different clothes."

Captain Chandler walked up. "All I have to offer is coveralls. Will that do? And how did you two get past me on the gangway? No one reported seeing you cross."

Marshal Johnson laughed. "Captain, I told you she was a slippery one."

Shayla elbowed him, but said, "Thank you Captain, coveralls will be fine. This potato sack I'm wearing is ready to be thrown overboard."

The Captain smiled. "As long as you aren't in it when it goes over, Miss McKnight."

Shayla grinned and said, "I'll try, but I can't make any promises," then she excused herself to the bathroom and picked up a folded garment as she went. Inside the cramped stall, Shayla wrestled herself into the navy, blue coveralls. She looked down. "Charming, simply charming." She flipped the latch and opened the door to find a long dingy hallway before her. She recognized the place, but it felt strangely empty, when suddenly behind her came a familiar voice.

"It's about time you got here. Abba sent me through and told me to wait. By the way, how are you? You look terrible. Your hair's a mess and that git-up your wearing is ugly."

Arms flew at Ressa, before she could duck Shayla squeezed her tight. "Oh, I was worried about you."

"Don't strangle me, already. I'm fine. Hey, you know that Beau guy, he's pretty nice. He told the local coppers to take care of me—or else."

Shayla pushed Ressa out to arm's length. "It seems they did a good job. You look wonderful."

"Yeah, a lady copper took me out to buy some 'more suitable' duds and she took me to lunch. She said I could order anything on the menu, but I hadn't heard of half of the stuff, so I just got a hamburger. It was de-lish! Believe it or not, we never got many of those." She launched right in to a different conversation. "Do you know if your momma's got hitched yet or not?"

"No, I don't and I need to get back. I'm sure she and my brothers have been worried sick."

"Must be nice to have people to worry bout cha."

"Yes, it is, but I'm also sorry they've been worried."

Ressa turned to look down the hall. "It's okay kids. You can come out now."

Five young, frightened faces peered down the hall.

Shayla gasped. "They're still here. We have to get them out." She glanced around, then pointed. "That's the closet we came out of after we first met."

Ressa nodded. "You mean when I yanked you through and into this mess?"

Shayla smiled. "I don't regret anything except being separated from you. I think we're supposed to go back in there. Kids, follow me and Ressa. We're going to try to get you out of this awful place."

Chapter 16

Who Are You?

Ressa, Shayla and the five other children entered the closet and stood in front of a smudged window. She pulled up the sleeve of her coveralls and wiped a small spot in the glass.

Tiptoeing behind her, Ressa asked, "What can you see, Shay?"

Shayla cupped her hands around her eyes and leaned in. "It looks like the same bathroom."

"Do you see anyone?"

Shayla squinted. "Wait, the door is opening and I see a person."

Ressa flapped her hands. "Start yelling! Knock on the window."

Shayla complied, knocking on the glass and shouting, "Help, can you help us? Can you open the window?"

The person on the other side came closer and

leaned toward the glass, it was a young man. "Shayla, is that you?"

"Yes, I'm Shayla. Can you help us? My friends are here with me."

The boy tried to push the glass, but it didn't move. "It's not a window, Shay, it's a mirror."

Her voice quivered. "What? On our side it's a window."

Ressa urged her. "Shayla stick your hand up for him to grab. That's what I did with you, but it pulled you in when you stuck your hand through."

Shayla shouted at the glass. "I'm going to try to reach you, but don't try to grab for my hand until it's on your side."

"Wait, what? Are you going to break the mirror?"

"Just wait." She turned to the group behind her. "Ressa, take my hand and you kids form a line holding hands. Hold tight and don't turn loose for any reason."

They all nodded.

Shayla stuck her free hand against the window, then held it on its side like a knife blade and worked her fingers through the glass. When her hand and wrist were on the other side, she yelled, "Now, grab my hand, brace yourself and pull hard."

The young man followed her directions. He placed one foot against the wall below the mirror and gripped her hand with both of his.

She shouted. "Now pull, hard!"

He tugged with all of his might. Shayla's arm and shoulder slid through the glass, then the side of her face came through.

The boy backed up and pulled again. Shayla's head and both shoulders cleared the mirror, her body lifted from the floor and started through, followed by Ressa's hand and arm.

When Shayla's feet hit the floor in the bathroom, she turned to the mirror and pulled Ressa all the way through, the others were coming through slowly when the boy saw what was happening, he grabbed on to each arm as it appeared through the glass.

When Ressa and the five other young people were in the bathroom with them, the young man shouted, "Shayla are you okay?"

She turned to him, her forehead furrowed. "Who are you? How do you know me?"

He patted his chest. "It's me, Benjamin."

Shayla lifter her hands. "Benjamin who?"

"Benjamin Perez."

She leaned toward him. "Benji, the little boy down the street?"

He laughed. "Yes, Benji."

"Benji, what are you doing here and how did you know it was me?"

"Abba sent me and Shayla, I would recognize you anywhere!"

At that moment, the bathroom door burst open. A man's voice filled the room. "This is the police, we're coming in!"

Shayla spun to face the door and stepped in front of the children.

Police, with guns drawn, stood in front of her.

One officer said, "Miss, a woman reported seeing a young man acting suspicious and she said he entered the ladies' restroom. Are you okay?"

"Yes, thank you, I'm fine, officer."

"Then why is your," he scanned down her coveralls, "outfit dirty and your hair all messed up?"

"It was human traffickers, officer, but this young man," she stepped aside to reveal Benji, "helped us escape. We couldn't have gotten away without his help."

Two policemen scanned the bathroom. "Where are the traffickers now?"

Shayla knew this was going to be hard to explain, but she felt a small wing at her ear. "They ran out that way." She swept her hand across the mirror and toward the rear window. "Benji, heard me yelling and came to our rescue."

Benjamin looked at her like, *what*? Then he turned to the officers and smiled. "Hi, I'm Benjamin Perez. I've known Shayla since I was five."

Shayla stepped aside again to reveal the five girls and one boy cowering behind her. "With his help we rescued this group of children."

Again, the bathroom door swung in. "Ressa? Ressa? Are you here?"

Ressa grabbed Shayla's hand.

One officer swung to meet the woman and pushed his hand out to stop her. "Who are you, ma'am?"

"I'm Ressa's mother, she was kidnapped seven years ago when she was five."

"Why do you think she's here now, ma'am?"

"A very nice man with a bird on his shoulder came to my home and told me to come here and I would find my daughter, Teressa. I got here as fast as I could."

Ressa stepped forward. "Momma, is it really you?"

The woman rushed past the officer's outstretched hand and threw her arms around the girl. "Yes, Ressa, it's me. I never gave up trying to find you." She wept into her daughter's hair.

"Ma'am, I'm sure you'll understand, we will have to take everyone down to the precinct and get statements. We'll need to verify your story."

Wet eyes turned toward him. "That's fine, I have my daughter back now. Do what you need to do."

The officer turned his attention to Benjamin. "Son, what were you doing here?"

"It was that man with the bird. He must have

seen what was going on and told me to get over here. My dad and I are just visiting Sallis, but when I heard Shayla's voice, I knew exactly who it was."

"Where's your father now?"

"He's a minister and he's going to perform a wedding here in the park in a few minutes."

"Benji, that's my mom's wedding. Do you remember that our dad was killed in an accident seven years ago? And Mom finally met this really great guy."

Again, the bathroom door flung open. "Shay-Belle, are you okay? What are police cars doing out here?"

The police looked at Shayla.

"It's my brothers. Come on in guys."

In walked Mican, Madelaine, Ashton and Bailey.

Ashton looked at her, head-to-toe. "I thought you were going to fix your hair. What did you do? Roll in the floor having a fit or something?" Then he saw the children behind her. "Who are the munchkins?"

Shayla laughed and pointed at the boy next to her. "Well, this munchkin is Benji Perez who used to live down our street from us, years ago."

Mican stepped forward. "Dude, you're tall enough to soap Mom's whole car window now and I bet you can spell better too."[xxii] Her brother looked at her and laughed. "But Shay, how did you get into such a mess?"

An officer with his gun now holstered barked an order into his lapel mic. "Set up a perimeter. We're looking for a child trafficking ring." Then he turned to Shayla's brothers. "Seems your sister, with the help of this young man, have rescued these six children from traffickers."

Shayla leaned forward and addressed the officer. "There's another guy, Duncan, who helped three others escape too. I'm sure he's taken them to a station by now."

"We got that report several minutes ago on an Amber Alert, but that was in a different city. How'd you know about that?"

Shayla lifted her shoulders. "The man with the bird!"

Ashton interrupted, "Officer, our mother's wedding is going to start any minute here in the park, can our sister come with us?"

Shayla added, "And can Benji stay? His dad's the minister?"

The officer placed his hands at his belt. "We'll need you both down at the station later, but I guess you can stay for the wedding for now."

Bailey stepped forward. "Not looking like that, she's not. Step into a stall and we'll swap clothes, we're about the same size. I don't have to be a Bride's Maid and I've got my makeup kit and hair styling gear with me."

Shayla turned to speak to the children. "Ressa will be with you, don't be afraid. Go with these nice policemen, tell them as much as you can about the people who held you and where you were held before you climbed through the window into here," and she winked. "Okay?"

The officers led the children and Ressa, with her mom gripping her arm, to a waiting ambulance to be checked out before being taken to the station.

Bailey shooed Shayla's brothers, Benjamin and Madelaine from the ladies' room. Minutes later, the girls had swapped clothes and Bailey had freshened Shayla's hair and makeup.

Bailey wheeled her around to face the now infamous mirror and announced, "Now you're a *Boat.*[xxiii] Let's get out of here."

The Wedding music started.

Chapter 17

This Letter Will Wait for Ten Years to Be Delivered

Dear Miss McKnight,

Today, we met for the first time, though you will not receive this letter for ten years, but in order for you to understand (when I am finally able to present this to you) I will attempt to explain.

Shayla, I have been a Christian since I was ten-years-old. About a year after my commitment to the Lord, he showed me pictures of myself as an infant, then as a child, all the way to manhood.

In the final picture, Abba showed me a beautiful lady probably in her early thirties. I was standing behind her holding a small child. At that time, he told me I would have a family, but *it would be a little while* and I was to be patient and to wait.[xxiv]

When I met you today, or ten years ago today, I instantly recognized you as the lady in the picture, but then to my amazement I learned you were only seventeen. Abba's words, *it would be a little while,* rang in my heart.

In prayer, I sought his guidance. The Lord assured me we would meet again, ten years from today. Though I was twenty-one at the time, he asked me to wait and to save myself for you and that you would do the same for me. He told me to pursue my career, but that he also had a plan for your life; so patiently, I have endeavored over the years to keep an eye on you and your career from afar.

I trust the Lord so much that I will wait/have waited for you. Even at age seventeen, Shayla, you are (were) the most remarkable young woman I've ever known. Your devotion to and trust of Abba was amazing. Your dedication to the children you were attempting to rescue was inspiring. Your fierceness in battle was moving, but to learn of your power in spiritual warfare was thrilling.

You were quite beautiful then, but you won my heart with your virtue; your beauty was only enhanced by your nobility of heart. You are truly unique and I am convinced you are the only girl/woman in the world for me.

Shayla McKnight, will you look away from this letter—at me down on one knee—and will you accept my proposal of marriage?

Your Hopeful Future Partner in Life,
Beau Johnson

Still NOT the End!

A Note to Parents: There is a Child ID App available on the FBI.gov website under Resources.

This App allows you to fill-in data about your child and keep it on your phone. In an emergency, it can be sent to any office or department you choose. This enables you to compile information and pictures before the pressure of an emergency, which in Jesus' name I pray never happens to you or your family.

I am not usually one to allow data about my family to be stored electronically for easy access, but in today's world, some actions are wise to take. Again, this data doesn't become the property of the FBI. It stays on your phone, unless you need to share it with authorities.

Please prayerfully consider taking advantage of this tool developed by the FBI.

Many Blessings!

June Whatley

My Story!

When I was sixteen my family took a cruise to Nassau, Bahamas. For us, that was a rare event. My parents were divorced, so Mom worked to support herself, my brother and I lived with our dad who was a blue-collar working man.

To my mom, status was important, so she saved and had arranged the trip. Since she couldn't drive, she had to rely on our dad for transportation, but truthfully, he would never have allowed us to go on vacation with her, without him. Mom was not always, shall we say, reliable.

So, on the cruise, she and I shared a small room, Dad and my brother shared the adjoining compartment.

One day on this trip my dad had taken my brother to the beach while Mom and I stayed on the ship. There was a Straw Market on the pier that I wanted to visit, it was in sight of the boat, so Mom allowed me to run down, to buy a purse. While I was shopping, I noticed a man in a white suit and a white straw fedora-style hat, watching me. Normally I was a very friendly, out-going person, but this man gave me the creeps.

I chose a purse and paid the sweet, cheery lady, who from her accent, I would guess was probably Jamaican. As I headed toward the end of the open shed, I noticed the man began to pursue me. He, the sales woman and I were the only people in the market at the time. The woman I had just paid saw what was happening and placed her large frame in the aisle blocking the man's way.

I glanced back over my shoulder and saw him trying to push past her in the narrow aisle as she shouted at him and waved her finger in his face. In the market, the rows were long so he couldn't go around to reach me. With the woman blocking his way, I broke into a run while she prevented him from passing. I reached the stairs to the ship and bounded aboard.

Later my dad and brother returned. Dad saw the purse and asked where I had gotten it. When I told him, he turned to my mother and shouted, "She could have been kidnapped!"

My father was very smart, but also had quite a temper and I tried never to cross him, so out of fear, I never told either of my parents about the episode and for about fifty years I never told a soul. I was in my sixties when I finally told my brother about the incident. Since then I have felt free to share my story, but also driven to try to educate young people—girls and boys—of the dangers that lurk, sometimes closer than we would like to think.

I regret not being able to thank my rescuer, but I assume that my escape was thanks enough to satisfy her.

I praise the Lord for the woman who was willing to stand between me and danger. Years later, I still sometimes pray for her and her family, though she is probably long since gone from this world. I also wonder if she had been abused earlier in her life and that was the reason she had stepped in to help me and perhaps that was the reason she had allowed herself to gain so much weight.

I have known abused women who have deliberately allowed their appearance to go downhill as a defense mechanism against sexual abuse. Please know, God can heal that fear and dread.

The Sleeper Awakens, Book 1 (Reading level, ages 8 and up)

Cloud Skimmers, Book 2 (Shayla is 12-years-old, @ ages 10 and up)

From the D.E.E.P., Book 3 (Ages 10 and up)

Whisked Away, Book 4 (Parental Warning: For upper Middle Grade to Young Adults)

Endnotes

[i] June Whatley, *From the D.E.E.P.*
[ii] June Whatley, *Cloud Skimmers*
[iii] *Cloud Skimmers*.
[iv] June Whatley, *The Sleeper Awakens*.
[v] Romans 3:25.
[vi] 1 John 2:2 & 4:10.
[vii] Romans 12:19
[viii] Luke 17:2.
[ix] Revelation 22:1.
[x] John 15:3, Psalm 103:12.
[xi] 1 Thessalonians 1:6.
[xii] Psalm 91:11.
[xiii] Isaiah 54:17.
[xiv] 1 Samuel 19:8.
[xv] Acts 13:22.
[xvi] Psalm 144:1.
[xvii] John 18:10-11.
[xviii] Proverbs 3:5.
[xix] Romans 12:19.
[xx] Mark 16:20.
[xxi] Isaiah 54:17.
[xxii] *The Sleeper Awakens*.
[xxiii] *Cloud Skimmers*.
[xxiv] *The Sleeper Awakens*.

Resources:

If you know of or suspect that someone is being trafficked, please notify authorities. If it were you, wouldn't you want someone to speak up?

http://humantraffickinghotline.org/

Call 1-888-373-7888 (TTY: 711)|*Text 233733 |Live Chat

U.S. Government Entities Combating Human Trafficking State Department: http://www.state.gov/g/tip/index.htm

Department of Homeland Security: http://www.dhs.gov/files/programs/humantrafficking.shtm

Department of Defense: http://ctip.defense.gov

Department of Justice: http://www.justice.gov/crt/crim/overview.php

Department of Agriculture:

Made in the USA
Monee, IL
06 August 2021

74521450R00104